# Children of Midgard

## By

## Siobhan Clark

Bretwalda Books, Unit 8, Fir Tree Close, Epsom, Surrey KT17 3LD
info@BretwaldaBooks.com
www.BretwaldaBooks.com
ISBN 978-1-910440-44-5

Printed and bound in Great Britain by
Marston Book Services Ltd, Oxfordshire

## The Children of Midgard

*The year is 961 and King Harald Bluetooth of Denmark has his gaze firmly set on the Western Kingdoms of Norway where his nephew Harald Greycloak reigns. Bluetooth has declared Greycloak as his vassal King of Norway and will claim the establishment of the Jomsvikings. In doing so he will solidify the order building a keep for the warriors he intends to use to create a fleet of men who will own the seas under his command.*

*However the order is older than one man's claim and consists of many who have their own destinies separate from the feuding monarchs. There are men of honor and worth and there are those who seek naught but power and privilege, searching only to prosper from the misery of others. There are tales of a legendary ring and child who is said to be the progeny of the All-Father.*

# 1.

The woman's heart was pounding in her chest, her legs ached from running but she knew she could not stop; the child was hidden and safe for now. Behind her she heard heavy boots crunching on the shore; the men were fast approaching and Liv realised she could not outrun them. It was like before when they had come for her husband and her guardian and now they were dead.

"Stop!" One of the men bellowed.

Liv froze despite her mind telling her to move, her skin goose flesh, the cool night air pricked her senses snapping her back into movement. They would surely catch her now but she would give nothing away she thought. Suddenly Liv was pushed to the ground, the gravel scraped her hands and face where she skidded along the uneven surface, two men stood either side of her heaving body and each roughly grabbed an arm. Hauling her to her feet Liv stifled a cry of pain as they proceeded to drag her back the way they had come.

"You will pay now!" One of the men growled in her ear.

Liv swallowed hard, she knew what these men would do, they were Jomsvikings. Mercenaries, assassins, and marauders; they had their own code and were fearless in battle. They selected their warriors through combat and were feared for their notoriety. The Jarl must have paid the men well to search for her; was he to stop at nothing she thought. She did not recognise either of the men but that meant little, the Jomsvikings that had been sent before to dispatch of her husband and guardian would be looking elsewhere, they did not give up easily once set to task.

"She had a horse…" One of the men turned to her. In the dark she could make out strong features and a dark beard. "Where is it?"

Liv swallowed. "Grani is lame I left him in the forest."

"Ha! Stupid woman calls her horse after Odin's steeds offspring? See I told you!" The other man snorted. Removing his helmet she could see a mass of wild untamed hair and a nose that had been broken and poorly set. A mouth of chipped teeth grinned at his comrade. "Women always think themselves so clever but you couldn't outrun us could you?"

The man spat in the sand and gruffly shook Liv's arm. The dark haired Viking guffawed and shrugged his shoulders. "We need no lame horse Grani or not. Walk!" He barked.

Picking up the pace the men strode towards the grassy field that ran alongside the shoreline. In the distance Liv saw a man on horseback with a lit torch in his hand. As they approached the rider jumped to the ground and walked towards them.

"Fetch me rope to bind her hands, I'll take her, the Jarl will want her swiftly. Get your horses." His deep voice snapped the orders at the two men who set about their leader's task without a word. Dropping Liv's arms they stalked off to their own horses tied to post hammered into the earth and gathered rope leaving her looking at the third man.

The leader too wore a helmet which he did not remove, Liv could not make out his features as the light of the torch danced between them, the only clue of what lay behind the battered and scratched surface of the metal was long brownish coloured hair. It was too dark to tell the colour of his eyes and she shuddered at the coldness of him.

"Where is the boy?" He growled.

"Dead…" Liv swallowed.

"You are unharmed?" The man lowered the torch to survey her. Her dress was ripped and covered in grit and mud. Her hair though braided had come loose and hung over her shoulder, it was the colour of bronze and streaked with flashes of gold from many days spent in the sunlight. He saw that her face was bleeding slightly from the grazes on her chin and cheekbone.

"Why do you care?" Liv whispered looking away to the two men who were returning with rope and a cloth sack.

"I don't…" He spoke dryly. His hand wandered to the handle of the axe tucked into his belt. Liv saw his fingers grip the shaft and felt fear rise in her throat.

Suddenly the man swung the torch into the face of the dark bearded Viking, a howl of pain erupted from his mouth before dropping to the ground. The leader of the men then swung his axe clipping the wild haired warrior on the shoulder who let out a low rasping breath of pain. Both men staggered in the dark groping for their own weapons and cursing their leader furiously.

Liv felt her hand being grabbed and pain shot through her fingers, roughly the man lifted her by the waist and threw her over the back of the horse. Jumping astride the beast the man kicked it into a gallop and headed for the forest. As they rode he shouted to Liv.

"Your horse?"

Righting herself into a seated position she pointed to a large fallen tree, there she had hidden Grani before attempting to flee on foot, the man pulled on the reins of his own horse and nudged it toward the tree. Behind the upturned blanket of root and earth Grani stood awaiting his master.

"Dismount!" The man barked at her. Obeying Liv did as she was bade and landed awkwardly on the ground. Stumbling towards Grani she felt her shoulder jerked away before she could reach the reins. "We take your horse. They will be looking for us, I leave mine here."

Once again the man jumped astride but this time extended a calloused hand to her. Liv withdrew taking a step away from the man.

"Take my hand or be dragged!" He said flatly.

Liv took a breath and stared at the dark circles of the helmet where eyes should have been. She saw nothing and wondered if this man might be some demon trying to trick her or take her for his own. She had heard tell of such mischief and had seen much in her own life to attest to the will of that other than men. Reluctantly she took his hand and felt herself being half pulled onto Grani's back behind the body of the Jomsviking leader.

"Hold fast we ride hard." The man pulled her arms about his waist and kicked Grani in the sides sharply. The horse grunted and proceeded on the path.

Quickly they made their way back to the settlement where Liv had first discovered the men had caught up with her. The owner of the tavern and tried in vain to help her escape unseen and she wondered what had happened to him and his wife, she had been sure she heard screaming from within the tavern's walls. The first rays of sunlight were beginning to break through the clouds covering the dawn. In the distance Liv could see a large ship moored beyond the settlements small harbor littered with small fishing vessels and the Chieftains small but sturdy skute.

Gripping the man's waist she felt revolted at having to hold him so closely and tightly. His rough cloak scratched at her face aggravating the cuts from her fall. She could feel the cold hard steel of the axe tucked into his belt against her arm and an idea formed in her head. Quickly she slipped her hand underneath his cloak and grabbed the weapon, pulling it free she pushed with all her might on his back shoving him forward on Grani and jumped from the galloping horse.

The jump from Grani's back winded her slightly, Liv struggled for breath but fought to control herself, gradually she rose to her feet and frantically searched for a route in which to run. The man had pulled Grani to a halt, turning in the saddle he spotted Liv and yanked on the reins of the beast. Grani whinnied and stamped his feet, shaking his black mane the horse reared and bucked at the commands of his rider. Liv thanked Odin for Grani's stubbornness and turned to run towards the grassy knoll to her right, from there she knew the forest grew thick before breaking out onto a rocky ravine. She could run there and hide, she would make her way not stopping until she reached the most northerly point of the land and from there she would either swim or drown. She cared not, all that mattered was the child was safe, grasping the heavy axe in her right hand she made for the knoll.

A shout rang out from behind her and turning quickly Liv saw the man dismount Grani and start after her. He was terribly quick for being large and strong; he gained on her despite the weight of his leather armour and sword strapped to his side. Liv cursed her weary legs from not picking up the pace but she had worn them out from her earlier attempts at escape.

"Liv!" The man called.

Stopping short Liv felt a cold shiver run down her spine. She knew that voice but how could it be, it was a voice from her past, but before her mind could recollect the man was upon her. Pushing her to the ground he loomed over her, grabbing her arm he twisted the axe from her grip and shoved her back onto the grass. The pain and harshness of his actions knocked the air from her lungs. In a moment of weakness, she raised her arm to her face to protect herself from the blow she guessed was coming. Liv had taken many beatings but refused to let this man deliver her her last. But the man drew a breath and took a step back.

'Control yourself!' The man chastised himself. He was outraged at his roughness with the woman. He had called out her name and she had stopped, had she recognised his voice he wondered, but then the rage had taken over. 'Can she not see we must make haste?' His mind raced.

"Get up." He said as softly as he could muster. "Please."

Liv dropped her arm and stared at the shadowy figure above her. Again he offered her a hand but refusing it she pushed herself to her feet. "Your Jarl will reward you well, twice I escaped and twice you caught me." She said bitterly.

"We need to get aboard that ship before the other men catch up with us." He swung an arm and pointed to the ship in the bay.

Liv squinted at the man. "You can reach the Jarl by foot."

"Start moving I won't ask again."

"You didn't ask." Liv said and placed one foot in front of the other slowly heading for the waiting Grani. Stroking the horse's neck she whispered softly to it before looking at the man.

The woman was causing him to feel, he did not enjoy what stirred in his chest and fought with all his might to not remove his helmet, he focused on the axe in his grip and breathed steadily.

"We can take the horse but move now." He spoke sharply and nudged both Liv and Grani towards the bay.

"Grani? Why? He does not belong to the Jarl!" Her voice was low but shook.

The man shook his head and pushed them onwards. "Keep walking."

As they skirted the path and started along the shoreline to an outcrop of rocks that stretched all the way to the ship, steadily they urged Grani onto the rocks and picked their way with care. Liv saw the man stroke Grani's nose gently and felt a pang of anger that he was so patient with her beast and so full of ire for her. She tore her gaze away from him and pulled her own dark woolen cloak about her shoulders. It had been gifted to her by a farmer's wife two seasons ago when her husband had been killed, her guardian had disappeared and Liv presumed he had been taken to the Jarl and either tortured or imprisoned somewhere. She felt sadness wash over her at the thought of the gentle old man withering away or worse crying out in agony until he met his end.

A group of seabirds cried out at the dawning of the amber sun rising in the twilight sky, they sounded to her like the squawking of a child her thoughts betraying her into thinking on her charge. It had wounded her heart terribly to leave the child but she had had no choice. She had to separate the child from the ring and had managed to do so but now it was her burden alone, the ring the Jarl sought was still concealed in the brooch her husband had made in the forge. So far it had remained uncovered though it bothered Liv that the Jomsviking has not asked her for it nor had he inquired about the boy.

Liv reasoned that the man was naught but a hunter, he had his prey what need was there for questions, he had been taken on to find her and he had completed his task. There was no more to do than deliver her to the Jarl. Liv looked again at the man, the daylight gave her better sight to try and recognise him. He stood tall, broad shouldered and strong, his hair was the colour of soft brown leather from beneath his helmet. He wore no rings on his fingers but she saw a gold band around his wrist and wondered if he wore it as a sign of wealth. His clothes though worn were of good quality and she thought him to be proud of appearance, he was certainly stern terse and hard. She saw nothing that revealed any more about the man except that his axe was indeed a fine weapon and the sword now slung across his back was heavy and inscribed with runes. She saw the rune for Odin and Thor, a bitter taste filled her mouth that he honored the same Gods as she did, that was where their similarity ended.

They stopped a few feet from the side of the ship and the Jomsviking turned to her. "When we board look no-one in the eye, speak to no-one, I will tell the captain you are mute and deaf so no man seeks to bother you. Cause me issue and you will be sorry." His words were commanding and unapologetic. He barely looked at her in the eye instead darting his glance from the shoreline to the ship where a man was waving them to come forward.

"You won't bind my hands?" Liv whispered facing the opposite direction from the crewman. He appeared small upon the deck of the large vessel.

"No. Move."

Liv stood fast. "Why not?" Her eyes narrowed and tried to pull the eyes of the man towards her. "Is this your ship?"

"You are mute!" He snapped and pushed Grani forward. Liv followed knowing there was little else she could do.

The crew member dropped a plank for Grani to climb aboard; the Jomsviking then took Grani to the hold, the crewman stood with his hands on his hips staring at Liv. Before the man could approach the Jomsviking reappeared and roughly pulled Liv to a chest on the deck of the vessel and pointed at her to sit. He still wore his helmet and cloak and in the better light Liv thought she caught a glimpse of pale blue eyes. She frowned slightly.

"We are to set sail." He said looking out over the horizon, gazing at the sky he nodded at the favorable morning and unstrapped the belt from around his waist. Dropping the cloak he motioned for Liv to shuffle off of the chest and sit on the deck. Into the sea chest he placed the cloak and sword. Rolling up the arms of his tunic he removed his helmet but turned away from Liv before she could see his face. Striding to the side of the ship he dipped the helmet into the water and poured the contents over his head. Leaning his forearms on the wood he paused to collect his thoughts before replacing the helmet and returning to the woman trying to peek at him beneath her lashes with curiosity. He realised he could not wear the armour for the entire voyage.

"You will avert your gaze at all times, I've told them you are a thrall so look at the ground never at me or make eye contact with the others, understand?" As he spoke he untied the straps holding the leather armour to his chest. The cuffs about his wrists remained though he twisted them and flexed his fingers. "I don't like giving orders twice so obey Liv."

He watched as the woman nodded and looked at her hands. Carefully he removed his helmet and tossed it into the chest. Liv did not glance up at him or move at all, it struck him that she was being utterly compliant, he felt rotten inside to be so terse with her. It was not how it was meant to be he thought but at this time he could not reveal himself though he doubted very much that when at last she knew who he really was she would even care. She had betrayed their oath and it had meant all to him. Suddenly it irked him spitefully that she had not known immediately who he was, how could it be she had forgotten him so swiftly.

Liv sighed, the man was intolerable, and she also suspected he was untrustworthy. He would not answer her questions. She knew full well that the Jarls lands were easily reached by foot, there was no need to set sail and there was little need to bring Grani with them. She loved her horse but was prepared to abandon him to the settlement, it was the way of things in her life, she could not hold on to anything that attached her to places or people for the loss of her husband and guardian had taught her that well. Liv resigned herself to silence, she would do as the man asked, she would be mute and deaf and compliant for soon enough the only sound to fill her ears would be that of her own screaming when at last the Jarl had her.

# 2.

Sleep eluded Liv as the ship made for open waters though her mind and body ached dreadfully from exhaustion. Men had gathered on deck and taken their positions at the oars, the Jomsviking had instructed her to sit near the prow where his back faced her. She thought it odd he would do this as she might easily have escaped over the side of the ship but she also saw the man at the rudder was watching her, Liv suspected the Jomsviking had made this man aware she was his captive.

Massaging her temples against the dull throb that had invaded her senses Liv sighed heavily. Her task had taken its toll, the constant evasion of the Jarls men and the danger she encountered being a woman on the run with a child had meant many sleepless nights, since her guardian had disappeared she was without counsel. For two years she had only her wits and guile to have gotten her and the boy this far and now she was captured. Her husband's cleverness in concealing the ring within the brooch on her cloak gave Liv hope but realising the men thought she was a thrall she tugged it from her shoulder and concealed it under her dress.

The touch of the jewel ignited a sensation of burning in her chest, she stifled a cough and watched as the Jomsviking turned his head slightly as she cleared her throat, she hated the weight of the ring. It had been draining her steadily over the last few months as the boy grew, Liv knew the time was coming when he would wear it and forever his fate would be sealed, she hoped it did not cause him as much anguish as it had her.

Liv looked at her hands and felt ashamed at the grime and muck under her fingernails. Her dress was tattered and torn and she knew not what her scratched and dirt smeared face looked like in the light of the new day. Smoothing her hands over her hair she felt the sea air had already tangled it; Liv grimaced a small smile to think she was safe enough from any man on the ship given what she must look like. It occurred to her that this was the first time in a long time she had cared, always she had kept her dress simple and her hair tied back, it had to be that she faded into the crowds. Her guardian had told her to be careful making eye contact and survey each gathering with a view that her and the boys' killer was there. Thinking back to the day when she had agreed to watch over her charge sent a stabbing pain of regret through her. Liv had wished for a very different life but the boy's mother had to be protected and they had failed when she died; then the boy had to be watched over as he was the last of his line, that was six years ago.

Suddenly the wind picked up and the Viking manning the rudder shouted at the men to pull in the oars and raise the sail. They did as they were commanded and returning to their wooden chests they took the opportunity to rest. The Jomsviking ignored the men and walked over to Liv with a skin. Averting her eyes she felt the skin drop into her lap.

"Drink." He ordered.

Liv took a sip of the stale water and felt her chest loosen a little.

"You are ill?" The man asked.

Startled Liv opened her mouth before clamping it shut and shook her head quickly.

"Good. My name is Gorm, look at my hands, should you need to ask for me use this hand signal." The man splayed his fingers in a wavering motion simulating the flight of a bird. "The men here all use this method when we fight… oft we cannot risk being heard. I will be watching… always."

Nodding her head Liv darted her gaze back to the wooden planks of the deck. She heard the man sigh and rub his face with his rough hands. She felt the skin lifted from her lap as he took a drink himself.

"You are not what I expected." Gorm said almost sadly. "I thought there would be more fight in you, mayhap it's all but gone, no matter…"

Liv restrained herself from looking up at the man and instead turned away from him angry that he made judgments about her.

'What right does he have?!' her mind screamed, 'What I have had to do!' instantly Liv chastised herself. Anger and grief from the tiredness she felt was overriding her usually measured mind, she would not let her captor rile her, she focused on the boys' face the last time she held him. Tears pricked her eyes as the memory of their last words; she had promised to return to him after hiding the ring but now all he could do was wait. Liv felt a dark ire surging within her, vowing silently that she would escape and return to the boy she channelled all her energy into forming a plan. She would not see the Jarls wrath yet, she would fight with every ounce of her being. The ring meant nothing to her; it was Liv's belief that the boy was powerful in his own right, it was naught but the greed of men that had forged the item to signify its wearers command.

Gorm looked at the woman he knew as Liv, his words had stung her and he goaded himself for being so petty, it was true he had expected her to fight harder however. She could have hit him with the axe while on the back of Grani but she did not, she submitted to his demands whilst on the ship and had uttered not one word. She looked tired and pale but still as beautiful as when they were young, as a Jomsviking he had seen what a hard life could do to a pretty face and was glad Liv had been saved from that. He wondered angrily how often she might have used that pretty smile to evade capture.

"You had a man?" He asked all too gruffly. He saw her nod hesitantly still turned away. "He is dead?" Again he saw her nod. "Then you are alone?"

Liv let out a breath and swallowed. She wondered now why he questioned her and felt frustration tangle her thoughts, what was his interest and why had he not asked about the ring, her mind raced. Defiantly she raised her head and stood stumbling slightly as her legs were unprepared for the movement of the ship.

"Sit!" Gorm growled at her clasping a hand on her forearm. "Eyes down."

Liv stood firm and turned her body to gaze out over the sea. "Take your hand off of me." She whispered.

Gorm dropped her arm as if it was aflame and stiffened. A smile crept over his mouth as he leant in to whisper in her ear. "So you are not yet beaten? Good...but do not defy me again." With a heavy hand he pushed against her should forcing Liv to be seated once again on the deck.

Watching the back of the Jomsviking Gorm walk away Liv speared Daggers into his flesh with her minds eye. She watched as he paused feeling her anger but shook it off and continued to his sea chest. Liv realised they were sailing away from the Jarls territory heading north but where was still as of yet unclear. She thought of her homeland briefly but fought against recalling any memory for what good could it possibly do her to look into the past again. Closing her eyes Liv allowed sleep to wash over her tired body.

When she awoke it was nightfall, the men were engaged in drinking from skins talking and playing dice games, the deck was lit by a few lamps and the sky was clear with a round full moon shining down on the ship. The waters had stilled and there was no movement, the sail had been taken down and the anchor weighed, Liv stretched and peered over the side of the vessel seeing nothing but water on the horizon. Looking back to the men she saw Gorm standing with his back to her talking with the man who had been at the rudder, they appeared deep in conversation Gorm nodded and Liv cast her gaze downwards quickly when he turned in her direction. Expecting him to walk over to her with more harsh words Liv tensed and awaited his arrival but it did not come; instead Gorm sent another smaller man to her with a small bowl of dried fish and a cup of water.

Accepting the meal Liv nodded fixing her eyes on the food. Chewing each mouthful slowly she relished the salted fish and savoured the water even though it had taken on a staleness. She had not eaten since the tavern in the settlement and then it had been a weak broth interrupted by the arrival of the Jomsvikings. When she had finished the meal Liv rested her head against the cool wood behind her, pulling her cloak about her shoulders she felt night air fresh on her tired skin, sleep threatened her once more. Her slumber was interrupted by the shouts of men, opening her eyes she saw two of the crew fighting surrounded by men who were slapping their thighs and laughing, the fight dispersed as quickly as it started and Liv saw it had been over a game of dice. Why men wasted their wealth on such things was a mystery to her.

She could not guess how long she had been sleeping but felt the weight of another blanket over her limbs looking down Liv saw that Gorm's cloak had been laid over her. Biting her lip she frowned at the gesture; why would he care to think of her comfort, Liv resigned herself to thinking that he wanted as good a reward as possible from the Jarl and should her health devalue her in any way it would cost the man. What good would she be to the Jarl if she was too sick or weak to interrogate she thought.

For the rest of the night she fought to stay awake, when dawn broke through the clouds that had gathered in the sky she folded the cloak and placed it beside her, the men rose at first light breaking their fast and waiting for their captains orders. Gorm did not approach her nor did any of the other men and Liv sat silently praying for an opportunity to present itself. She must escape she thought. Suddenly a rough hand yanked her to her feet, a scowl bore down on her and from the knotted fair hair and beard Liv knew it was not Gorm, her arm felt like it was in a vice and despite her efforts she could not pull away from the man.

"He says you're a slave? Don't look like any I've ever seen!" The man clenched his fingers on Liv's arm watching with a grin as she winced in pain. "Speak!"

Liv shook her head and shakily pointed to her throat, if this was a test sent by Gorm she would not fail. The man looked at her puzzled swinging a glance around the deck, Gorm was not in sight. Roughly he dragged Liv towards the hold, none of the men looked up from their tasks, panic rose in Liv's throat as she realised Gorm's lie was the perfect opportunity for a man such as this, thrall status offered women no protection. Trying to steady her breathing Liv's thought of her small Dagger in her boot that the Viking had not checked for and thanked the God's. The mans pace quickened as he reached the plank leading down to the hold, Liv could smell the odour from the animals and prayed that Grani was safe and that he might stamp his hoof into the mans head given half a chance, his grip loosened as he swung her to his face.

"Since you can't speak you can't shout for Gorm." The words slithered from his leering face.

The man raised a hand hitting Liv on the jaw, her head buzzed with the force from the blow and she staggered back, nausea overwhelmed her as she sank to her feet. Straining to keep upright she fell onto the wooden decking landing hard on her injured face. Forcing her eyes open she looked up at the figure before her blurring into many shapes, as it loomed over her in a squatting position it pulled at her hair, then just as Liv prepared for another blow a second figure appeared behind the man. The bearded figure turned but it was too late the second man had raised his fist and smashed Liv's attacker repeatedly in the face. Falling onto her back Liv felt the hold spinning, her eyes rolled into the back of her head, strong hands lifted her shoulders and a voice whispered in her ear.

"Liv? Speak!" Gorm's tone was hushed but filled with anguish; he was enraged that Freki had attempted to take Liv when Gorm had strictly forbidden the men to go near her.

The darkness of the hold prevented Gorm from seeing how injured Liv was, he cursed his earlier attitude towards her, lifting her over his shoulder he climbed back onto the deck and laid her in the spot he had ordered her to remain. The jaw appeared unbroken though a dark purple bruise was beginning to work its way across her face. Freki must have caught her ear as a thin droplet of blood trickled from within. Looking about the deck Gorm glared at the men who had done nothing to stop their comrade from his intentions, cursing his plan to call her a thrall Gorm scratched his head before swearing loudly balling his fist and punching the wood of the deck.

Slowly Liv stirred and strained to open her eyes. She could tell she was no longer in the hold but pain throbbed in her left ear and her jaw ached, there was a taste of blood in her mouth but using her tongue to trace her teeth she found none broken or missing. Swallowing she pushed back on her elbows and attempted to sit but the spinning sensation swept over her once more and she felt a hand gently pushing her down.

"Please rest. We will depart the ship by the evening, nod if you understand." Gorm spoke as softly as he could muster. He watched as she nodded, her eyes struggling to focus he wished he had never told her to avert her gaze from him, he longed for nothing more than the green opal eyes to look at him with an assurance all would be well. "I will seek out a healer if you have not yet recovered."

Liv shook her head and winced at the pain. She could not allow a healer to look at her, they would surely wish to inspect the rest of her body for injury and she could not allow that to happen. Groaning she raised her hand to the blurred figure before her and rested a palm on his forearm.

Gorm started at the touch of her hand; pulling back he reached for his cloak neatly folded into a square and tucked it behind her head. He waited for a moment until she appeared to have slipped into unconsciousness and stalked toward the hold.

Freki still lay in a bloody mess on the floor; the crewman had dragged his knees up to his chest both hands cupping the smashed nose on his face.

"You knocked out my teeth and broke my nose!" He spat.

"You were warned not to touch her!" Gorm roared.

"She's naught but a thrall what difference would it make." Freki whined grimacing at the pain radiating his face. His eyes began to water as blood and drool dripped from his chin.

Gorm bent down and grabbed fistfuls of the man's tunic dragging him to his feet. "You injured her, she's my property, you will pay one way or another." He growled into the man's face.

Freki squinted at the rage in Gorm's eyes, gulping he cursed himself for going against the wishes of the Jomsviking, this man was not to be trifled with. Though he had never heard of Gorm he recognised the hardness of character and from the battle scarred face and hands Freki guessed this man had seen many a battle.

This did not bode well for himself he thought.

"I have coin in my chest." Freki stammered.

"Get it. If you so much as glance at her before we reach the township I break the rest of your teeth and your jaw." Gorm released his grip and watched the man stagger over the ramp and out into the morning light. "What am I doing?" He sighed.

Suddenly the shout for the men to man the oars came and Gorm shook off his fury proceeding to his chest. Taking his seat he watched as Freki approached and tossed a bag of silver to him before stalking back to his own chest. The captain at the rudder raised and eyebrow but Gorm was in no mood to explain and darkened his gaze with a frown. Shrugging the captain roared for the men to drop their oars and pull.

It was still morning, the sky was grey, rain was on the horizon and not a breath of wind could be felt. Liv dreamt of her past as a youth, of a kindness she had known and the face of one she had loved, when she awoke the day had turned to early evening and misting of rain had dampened her clothes. Swallowing back the pain Liv felt tears well in her eyes as she relived the memory of her dream. Rolling on to her side she struggled to regain her balance pushing with all her might she rose to her feet. Lurching to the side she felt her knees buckle but before she fell a pair of arms caught her.

"Raise your hood." Gorm said. "We have reached the township. Let me lift you onto Grani and rest until I say."

Liv nodded and covered her face with her hood. She felt Gorm raise her over his shoulder before he took the reins of Grani and led them over the side of the ship. Slowly Gorm placed one foot in the stirrup and patiently helped Liv into the saddle; satisfied that she would not fall he budged Grani to move forward.

"Gorm!" A voice rang out from the ship.

Turning Gorm saw the captain and stopped in his tracks. "Ragnar?"

"Wait!" The captain bounded along the deck and leapt over the ship of the ship now moored in the harbour. "The woman she is well?"

"I think she needs a healer."

"Best be on your way and quick, you have a man here?"

"Yes why?"

"Freki is still smarting from your beating, one of the men told me he plans to get his coin back from you, now I know you can take care of yourself but your cargo says otherwise." Ragnar jerked his head of wiry red hair towards Liv. The captain had pale blue eyes that saw through many a guise and he figured this woman to be no thrall no matter how convincing Gorm's story was. "With the Jarls men on your back you don't need the likes of Freki doing the same."

Liv stiffened as her ears picked up on the conversation between the two men. Could she have heard the captain correctly she wondered. Her heart started to beat rapidly in her chest; if this man had caught her for what purpose could it be if not to return her to the Jarl?

"Quiet Ragnar." Gorm hissed darting his gaze around the men loitering on and about the ship. "I thank you but we will be well. I am to meet with my man now and we depart the township in the morn…Freki is no threat and I doubt the Jarl has knowledge of what has happened yet. Can I trust you to say nothing if they should come looking?"

"What would I say?" Ragnar shrugged. "That some Viking came aboard with a battered wench? Happens all the time, mayhap you are some trader selling a thrall at market. My men change often, Freki does not sail with me again."

Gorm nodded and lifted Freki's coin sack from his belt tossing it over to the captain. Ragnar caught the sack with both hands and feeling the weight nodded and winked at Gorm before turning and walking back onto the ship.

"Come Grani." Gorm pulled on the reins and started back along the path.

From beneath the heavy hood of her cloak Liv found the courage to seek a peek at the man guiding her horse. His own hood was down and he did not wear his helmet. As he pulled on the reins he turned his head this way and that searching the crowd. Liv saw a strong square jaw bristled with short hair, his nose was straight, a series of small scars scattered over his jaw and neck as if some claw had attacked him and left its mark. She could see no more and as Liv strained against the pain in her head she saw Gorm raise his hand and heard a shout from someone in the distance.

# 3.

The township of Gulafjord was bustling, the harbour strained against the swell of bodies pulling their carts and wares strung over shoulders; Dag weaved in and out of the crowd along the quayside littered with small vessels and larger ships. His humour was high this evening, he had secured them lodging on the outskirts of town where no one would think to look should Gorm have made any new enemies on the way and Dag reasoned that it was entirely possible given the task at hand.

King Harald Greycloak, grandson of Harald Fairhair, hailed from Syngfylki and the region had prospered in his reign, in a few days time Jarls would convene for the Thing debating over taxes and the concerns of their people. Harald Greycloak was the son of Eric Bloodaxe who had been next in line despite the many sons' of Fairhair battling for rights to the throne.

Upon the death of his father Greycloak and his brothers allied their forces with that of his grandfather fighting many battles and being the eldest son Greycloak held most of the power he and his brothers gained after the defeat of King Haakon of Norway. Greycloak had been born into a dynasty at war with themselves. Though now he had been proclaimed vassal King of western Norway by his uncle Harald Bluetooth of Denmark.

Recently there had been talk within the ranks, grumblings that Bluetooth was offering land and ships if the Jomsviking's were to swear allegiance to him. Though thier code of conduct forbade dissent there were many who bit back at the rumours that Bluetooth had proclaimed the order as being his creation. In truth the Jomsvikings were older than this. The one thing that was agreed upon amongst the men was the need of a larger citadel for the order of the Jomsvikings, currently they held residence in the great tower on the shores of a lake laden with crafts of many sizes and descriptions. To grow in number and power they had to lay claim to a larger more dominating fortress which had been promised by Bluetooth.

Many ships had arrived during the course of the day, Dag watched as the cargo's containing fine silks and cloths, spices and exotic foodstuffs were unloaded. Some ships carried fine looking steeds of the like the Arab men favoured, some carried slaves for the market which had stuck in Dag's throat. He neither appreciated nor respected the slave status; who could allow themselves to be treated so unkindly he often wondered, it was not a life and better the person sold into it ended it swiftly. Men shouted to one another preparing for trade in the township and organising meeting places to drink and eat, some were drawn to the women milling around the carts and storehouses looking for their own business. As dusk began to fall Dag saw lamps being lit and the harbour took on murkier tone, deals could be made with those who avoided the light of day, coin exchanging from hand to hand for passage onto ships leaving in the morning.

Dag had known Gorm since their enlistment in the Jomsvikings, the two men were similar in their skills and prowess but very different in demeanour, where Gorm was serious and reserved in temperament Dag was loud and brash seeking the joke in every situation and enjoying the mischief he could incur on his comrades. This had been the case at least until Gorm had approached him some weeks ago after a messenger had sought him out. Dag hoped that the woman Gorm was after was worth the trouble that would soon be on their tails. In his mind, no woman ever was worth the trouble, he took maid's, servant's, whores; and whoever else smiled or batted an eyelash his way, no female had yet to convince him to settle down and in truth why should he? So far with the Jomsvikings he had amassed his own wealth, of which he had carefully divided before this expedition, none having to pay for a woman's upkeep. He fought many a battle and won his right to die well and enter the halls of Valhalla, what need did he have of a mortal wife when the riches of the afterlife would be much sweeter.

A roving eye drew Dag's attention to a comely woman struggling with a sack, he watched for a moment with an amused grin as she tried time and again to lift the load over her shoulder, puffing she swept a hand across her brow and caught his gaze. Tucking his thumbs into the leather of his belt about his tunic Dag swaggered towards the woman.

"How come you find yourself here with such a load?" He smiled.

The woman tilted her head catching the glint in the man's eye. Warily she looked him up and down from his dark hair and rugged features she could tell he was no fisherman or farmer, she saw instantly he was a warrior and drew a breath. "My husband waits for me over there." She replied meekly.

Dag threw a look over his shoulder, as he turned he knew she would catch a glimpse of his heavy sword strung across his back. "Really? And he leaves you here to struggle?"

"Uh yes, I'll be on my way." The woman blushed.

"Sure I can't offer you a hand?" Dag dazzled the woman with his straight even smile. She blushed further, he thought this was again far too easy, he knew she had no husband here or anywhere. Catching her fire him a sideways glance he saw the brown of her eyes and the sharpness of her small features. Lifting the sack he threw it over his shoulder with ease and offered the woman an arm. "Where to?"

"You are a Viking?"

"Of a kind."

"What kind?"

"The paid for and don't ask questions kind." He grinned.

"Thank you for your help but…"

Dag rolled his eyes and rubbed his chin. "No need to fear me woman, I offer help, where to?"

"The tavern." The woman pointed to a wooden outbuilding some feet from where they stood. "I didn't have far to go." She smiled and pulled her cloak tighter over her dress. "We don't see many such as yourself here."

"Am I so different?"

"Ja, you look like you've seen many a fight, the raiders and traders have that look too but you're different, your weapons for a start. The sword is larger than any I've seen and you have Daggers all along your belt."

"You see much and talk much too, tell me is there aught to keep the words falling from your mouth?" Dag laughed and winked at the young woman enjoying the small smile spread over her lips.

Dag noted she wore the garb of a serving wench and wondered if she worked the rooms as well. Her face did not wear the look of a whore, but still it made little difference to him. Gesturing for the woman to walk he darted his eyes amongst the figures of the crowd, in the distance he saw a tall man in a dark cloak pulling a horse alongside, dropping the woman's sack he raised a hand and shouted at Gorm.

The woman dropped to her knees by the sack and gathered the vegetables that rolled from its opening. "Nei, nei!" She cried.

"My apologies!" Dag laughed and helped her gather the roots and saw the sack also contained dried meat.

"Gods above he will tar my hide!" She shot a worried look to the tavern and then to Dag.

"Who will?" Dag stood and looked about him for a sign of an angry man.

"My brother, he owns the tavern, I've already cost him and now the food is covered in muck. Pray I wash it off afore he see's." She raised her head briefly and stuffed the contents into the sack before struggling to lift the load once more.

"Your brother?" Dag took the sack and the arm of the woman before quickening his pace. Standing outside the door of the tavern he glanced inside. "Is he there?"

"No. I best be gone, thank you and well… no thanks at all!"

"Hah!" Dag laughed out loud before catching the woman's arm as she disappeared over the doorway. "Your name?"

"Gytha. Why?"

"Mayhap I return this evening and spend a coin or two?"

"As you wish but… this place is trouble it may be best you stay away." Nervously the woman looked away before wrestling her arm free leaving Dag's sight.

Shrugging Dag turned about and set off towards the spot he had seen Gorm approaching from. Absently he felt a little anger towards the brother of the young woman, the man obviously intimidated her,

Dag was not fond of the ways men could do this to women but he knew her not and resolved to let the matter rest in his mind until he saw her next and if he saw her again. There was every chance Gorm would want them to remain completely hidden from sight until the morn.

Noticing Dag making his way towards them it had not escaped Gorm's attention he had been speaking with a woman, Gorm sighed and wondered if his friend ever kept his mind on anything else. He was pleased to see his friend though and knew that he would have made the arrangements they had spoken of before he left. He had told Dag as much as he dared to, he knew his friend had suspected there was much more to the tale than hunting down a woman who had been treacherous in her betrayal of the Jarl. In fact that was the Jarl's lie alone, Liv had never been in his service or ever met him, and the Jarl wanted the ring.

The legend he had known of ever since he was a child, sitting round the fire pit in the hall of his people listening to their Seer, had found its way to ears of men. All who heard tell about the ring or had glimpsed upon it craved it, apart from Gorm. It sickened him that greed could destroy a person and he could not understand why Liv had given up her life to protect it. He knew not where on her person she had concealed it and cared not he had to deliver her to one man who could set the matter to rest. As far as Gorm was concerned the ring had to be destroyed.

"Gorm!" Dag laughed and slapped the man on the back. Looking at the woman on the back of the horse he raised an eyebrow. "She is ill?"

"Ja, some fool attacked her on the ship, we may have need of a healer."

"Mmm, mayhap. I have lodging for us, best we make haste, the owner of the house will gone for days. When we arrive I'll look for a healing woman." Dag darted a look at the woman as she moaned slightly hunching her shoulders as she sat weakly on the back of the horse.

"Best we move." Said Gorm.

Liv struggled to keep herself upright. She heard a man talking with the Jomsviking and furrowed her brow painfully as she tried to remember the conversation he had had with the ship's captain. Where were they going, why had the man taken her and who was this new voice she could hear? The two men clearly knew one another and their tone was friendly but urgent. Peering from beneath her hood she saw the new figure walking with Gorm, he had long dark hair and an equally broad shape to Gorm's, he flickered a look behind him and she saw a strong face, his beard was dark but short as if he had neglected to shave his whiskers for a few days. He smiled at her and she saw a spark in his dark eyes, she recognised the charm he exuded and sighed warily. He also wore a heavy sword on his back, his clothing was practical but well made, in the dusk and lamplight the blade glinted causing her to shiver.

"Your woman peeks from beneath her hood. All will be well…"

"She was told to keep her gaze down!" Gorm growled but felt a little tension lift from his shoulders that curiosity was awakening her.

"What woman can do as she's told?" Dag grinned. "And why down?"

Gorm scowled at his friend as they made their way from the harbour and started along a track skirting away from the township. The crowd thinned and became the odd group of men wearily carrying sacks and pulling carts or staggering fools who had spent or lost thier coin heading back to his ship to rest his broken head.

"She doesn't know, and keep your voice low, this way?" Gorm jerked his head to the path before them and Dag nodded.

"We are some paces from the house." Dag lowered his tone. "Why have you said naught?"

"There was no time to explain."

"What explanation would be needed when she saw your face?"

"She has not recognised my voice, mayhap she has forgotten me altogether, would be no bad thing now."

Dag grunted and peered back at the woman. "Bothersome woman, you save her skin and say nothing? Mayhap your pride is wounded Gorm?"

"Nay."

"Humph, ja I think it so. How many years have passed since you saw her last?"

Gorm tightened his grip on the reins. "Over six years."

"And you think she would know you by voice? In that time you have changed much, you are an older man now, even I would sound different to my mother's ears where she still living." Dag pointed to a small wooden structure nestled between a crop of stables and store houses. "Here, isn't much to look at but will suffice for now. Tis warm and clean and dry, there is food. Do you want me to look for a healer?"

Gorm looked at the ramshackle buildings, they were in need of repair but would indeed do for the duration of their stay, straightening his back he shook his head. "Nei, you take her inside I will look for a healer." Gorm handed Grani's reins to Dag and walked towards one of the larger square buildings where a little smoke was drifting from the thatch roof. The light misting of rain that had fallen during the day had dried and the path was firm beneath his feet. "Dag?" Gorm called back to his friend.

"Ja?" Dag raised his head slightly, his hand still stroking the horse's nose.

"Keep your hands to yourself!"

Dag roared with laughter, it was good that his friend saw fit to shed his grimness and jest with him, he would indeed keep his hands to himself if the woman still meant anything at all to Gorm.

Reaching up he pulled Liv from Grani's back and carried her into the small house. Once inside Dag laid her on the long table by the small fire pit and lit a lamp, pulling a bench aside he drew back her hood and saw she was staring at him wide eyed. The woman's face was scratched and bruised, Dag whistled at the markings wincing as he realised the blow from the man Gorm had spoken of must indeed have been heavy, lifting a hand he gently tilted her chin to further expose the bruising.

"Are you still in pain?" He asked.

"Some." Liv rasped.

"Gorm has gone for a healer." Dag said folding his arms across his chest.

"I don't need one. What does he plan for me?"

"Not for your concern right now." He looked at her green opal eyes, they were shaped like the sleek felines in the harems he had visited in the southlands, her lashes were dark and she looked something other than Norse. Her hair was of a bronze hue rather than the golden shades of his women. "Where are you from?"

"Nowhere." Liv struggled to sit and shuffled from the table to the bench across from Dag. "Why am I allowed to see your face?" Holding her head in her hands she balanced her elbows on the lip of the wooden table.

"Best you and Gorm speak about that. Besides is this not a fine face to look upon?!" Dag chucked slightly to himself. "I'll fetch you a drink."

Crossing the small room Dag lifted a clay pitcher and a wooden cup from a shelf, pouring the water Liv licked her lips and drank greedily enjoying the crispness of the fresh liquid, filling the cup for a second time Dag watched as the woman looked up at him and thanked him with her eyes as she drank. 'Gods above.' He thought 'what a fool Gorm is being!'

"Thank you." Liv said.

Dag nodded but suddenly the door swung open and a large figure filled the entrance. Liv immediately looked down, Dag looked first at his friend and then to the woman who averted her eyes from his friend.

"Give me strength!" Dag muttered.

"There is no healer nearby." Gorm grunted. Walking over the table he lifted the pitcher and drank. With a jealous look he glared at Dag and then to the woman. "I see she is much recovered anyway." He growled.

Dag shrugged his shoulder and rolled his eyes. "Needs be you two talk and swiftly, I'll return in an hour, we must rest well this night."

"Where are you headed?"

"A tavern, I have an errand to run. There may be a healer there, she needs one." Dag smirked and stood. Lifting the oil lamp to Gorm he whispered. "Mayhap this will shed a little light on the situation?"

Gorm grabbed the lamp and set it on the table angrily swearing at his friend. Dag shook his head pausing at the doorway, he was loyal to his friend but if they had any chance of succeeding further the woman could not be forced to continuously look at the ground, swallowing he made a decision.

"One hour my friend… mistress?" Dag could tell the woman was listening keenly. "Would you not look upon the face of the man you know as Ari?" Dag slammed the door behind him and walked swiftly back along the path they had taken together some short time ago. He did not look back for he neither wished to see his friend pursue him or the fist he knew he had earned.

# 4.

Gorm's jaw hung slack, the room seemed to chill though the fire was lit, he stood rigidly staring at the door Dag had closed. Sagging his shoulders he turned to see Liv standing looking at him. Her face was blank, her eyes wide and full, her hands clenched at her sides she mouthed something he could not hear. Her lips formed his name.

"Sit." He said.

"No."

"Please." Lifting his hands he gently approached her and lowered his palms. "Liv…"

"No. Who are you? Gorm? You cannot be Ari." Her voice was flat and dry; Liv heard herself speak but did not recognise her tone. Her chest ached and her heart tore in two, it could not be him she thought. But as she looked at the man's face a cold realisation hit her, she had been lied to, this was Ari.

The man before her was tall and strong, his hair was longer than she remembered, his eyes were sharp and blue like the pale winter skies. His face was as handsome as she had always known him to be but for the small trails of scars across his jaw and neck. Crossing the space between them she lifted her fingertips to his face before pulling away.

"How is it you are here?" She whispered.

Ari sighed misunderstanding her meaning. He had seen in her eyes she was amazed that he stood before her, why did she think she would never see him again, she appeared to be shaken by his very living. "I have to take you home."

Liv shook, she could not go back, there was nothing there for her. "No."

"We must…"

"No!" Balling her fists she let her anger spew forth. "How could you treat me that way? Taking me your prisoner? The ship? Why would you do that?!"

"You know!"

"What?" Liv let her confusion spread across her face.

Ari took a step back, his anger rose and he lifted the pitcher throwing it violently into the wall of the room. It smashed and water splashed on the earthen floor. Breathing heavily Ari dragged his hands through his hair before tearing off his cloak and throwing it on the table.

"You have the ring?" He barked at her.

Raising her eyebrows Liv felt nothing but disappointment. It had come, the reason he wanted her, he wanted the ring.

"You cannot have it."

"You will give it to me." He hissed at her. Facing her he leant into her face and looked her in the eye. "Where is it?"

"You… are not the Ari I once knew." Liv spat back with venom.

"No you are right. You destroyed that man some years ago."

Liv took a sharp breath and narrowed her eyes. She did not know from where his hatred sprang, did he not know she had been lied to by the one who had helped her all this time? Why had he come for her, to take her to their homeland but asking for the ring made no sense? "I did nothing to you…" Her eyes watered and she fought the sting of the tears.

"Is that so? You made an oath, then ran! You took this foolish errand and for what to escape me? Then I discover you took another man? You have no heart Liv."

"What?" Liv stammered not quite believing what Ari was saying.

"I will take you home, you will hand over the ring and be done with this, from there go live whatever life you choose I care not." Ari angrily sat on the bench covering his mouth with his hand. He was enraged at himself he could not believe the words that fell from his mouth.

Liv stood shaking. She wanted to run from the room, she wanted to jump upon Grani's back and ride hard out into the night, she fought the urge to scream. The child flickered into her mind and she thanked the Gods Ari had not mentioned him, she had lied about his death and Ari seemed to believe her.

Fatigue and shock took over and Liv fell to her knees, a great sob broke through her chest and tears fell heavily from her eyes. "I didn't know Ari… by the Gods I never knew!" She cried.

With a puzzled expression Ari looked at the woman on the floor before him. Her beautiful face covered by her hands, her sobbing tore at his heart and his anger faded. Kneeling beside her Ari wrapped his arms around Liv and breathed in her scent. She was exactly as he remembered her, how could he have been so vile to her he wondered, she was still his Liv she had not changed.

"Why Liv? Why did you run?"

Breaking free from his embrace Liv looked into the eyes of Ari. "He told me you were dead."

"Who told you this?"

"Harvardr… but now he is gone… dead I think. The Jarls men took him." Liv wiped her eyes and looked sadly at the floor. She could not understand why her guardian would have lied to her about Ari, what reason could he possibly have had to do so.

"Liv… please never look away from me again, I am sorry." Ari lifted her chin with his finger. Gently he stroked her hair from her face and offered a weak smile.

"Ari I swear if I knew you were alive I never would have left, never agreed to carry this burden… I had no choice."

"Liv we have much to discuss, I am uncertain where to start, but we must go home." Ari lifted her to her feet and gently guided her to sit on the bench. "First tell me why you do not wish to return?"

Liv sighed and pulled her cloak from her shoulders, the room was beginning to spin around her and there was a buzzing in her ears as if the room were filled with dozens of gadflies. "I'm so tired Ari, please let me sleep, then we might talk awhile. I have so much I want to say… to explain… I don't want your hatred." Her voice trembled as she spoke, a cold sweat broke across her brow and her hands shook.

Ari nodded he could see she was in no state to continue. Standing he walked to a pallet in the far side of the room and arranged the bedding furs, returning to Liv he guided her to the makeshift bed and watched as she drifted off to sleep. He wondered how far pushed into exhaustion she had become and how much was down to injury. His patience was thin and he struggled with the silence in the room. Resigning himself to waiting for Dag's return he quietly picked up the broken fragments of the clay pitcher and left the room. Outside the dwelling the cold night air was crisp and fresh, Ari could hear Grani in the stable and wandered to the outbuilding to check on the horse, the evening was silent save for the snorting of Liv's beast.

"Shh Grani your mistress rests as should you." Ari stroked the horse's nose. He removed the saddle and blankets from its back and lifted a bale of hay into the pen. The horse chewed on the dried grass keeping one eye on Ari all the time. Finding a small stool Ari took a seat and rested his head in his hands.

'Why would Harvardr lie?' He wondered. Ari considered there was much that the old man had omitted telling him, why would Liv spend the last six years on the run protecting a jewel and a child that was not her own, she had been attacked by Jomsvikings, pursued by the Jarl and his men. She had seen her husband killed and thought Harvardr captured or killed. Was a cursed ring worth protecting so fiercely he thought? He had asked her for it and she refused, but she did not wear it and so had not succumbed to the power it held, Ari began to wonder how much of the legend was true. An agonising thought entered his mind; how had the child died and how had Liv taken the death? He desperately wanted her to awaken and tell him all that had happened, he wanted to explain his anger and hoped she would understand, he did not want her to think of him as a murdering violent warrior paid for and unquestioning. He did not want her to believe he was merely a Jomsviking.

Ari felt for the pouch tied to his leather belt and the necklace inside. He had had it made for her when they were young. It was a simple amulet on a thin chain. He had discovered it next to her pallet with the other women thrall's after she had gone missing, it had wounded him terribly to think she had cast it aside so easily but if she believed him dead it explained much. Had she nursed a broken heart all these years he wondered, was there room for either of them to love one another again. From the moment his captain had received the word to hunt her down Ari had felt nothing but anger and sought an answer to the one question that had haunted him all these years; why? Now he knew Ari was uncertain what any of it meant.

It would take many nights before they reached their own settlement. Ari hoped that Dag would return with another horse thus they stood a better chance of arriving earlier than expected.

Dag walked into the tavern with a sense of unease, there was something amiss here, the men drinking were all too quiet and the maid scurried from table to table instead of working the room for an extra coin or two. He saw the young woman called Gytha carrying a large metal tray loaded with roasted meat, vegetable's, breads and cheese. Watching her he saw a worried frown on her face as she reached a table where two men sat with their backs to him and a third facing the doorway. The men were clothed in the same garb, matching cloaks slung about their shoulders, their swords still strapped to their backs and the third man facing him held a small Dagger in his twitching fingers.

Recognising this tactic he quickly looked away, spotting a passageway leading to the kitchens Dag disappeared from the men's sight, standing in the shadows he awaited Gytha. She seemed to be taking longer than he liked and when at last she walked towards him he saw she was rubbing her right arm. Stretching a hand from the darkness of his corner Gytha started and raised a hand to her mouth.

"You?!" She whispered. "What are you doing here?"

"Who are those men?" Dag jerked his head to the taverns hallway.

"What is your name… you are a Jomsviking aren't you?" Her voice trembled.

"Dag and yes I am… why ask?"

"They were asking about a Jomsviking but they did not give your name. Please you must go, my brother is already seething that they are causing the men to drink more cautiously if he see's you here he'll be furious." Gytha swung her head back and forth along the passageway looking for signs of her brother.

"What name did they give you?"

"I think it was Garm or Gorm... I can't remember my mind was elsewhere, one of them grabbed my arm... another sorry bruise." She whispered the last sentence and Dag stiffened.

"You are right I must go..." Dag felt alarm rising at the Jarls men looking for his friend. They might be strangers here and hidden themselves in the small steading outside of the township but that meant nothing if they asked the right person, at this moment that might be Gytha. "Your brother mistreats you?"

"He has a fear of healers... many do... but I have no choice." Gytha hushed her tone as a maid walked past them scowling as she went before seeing Dag and raising a small flirtatious smile.

Gytha rolled her eyes heavenward and Dag smirked before allowing the seriousness of the situation take over again. "A healer? Mayhap I have need of you, tell your brother a man came by and will pay good coin for your services, meet me in the stables behind the storehouses."

"No coin would be enough." Gytha's brother's hunger for prosperity was well known.

"Gold coin, for your time here tonight and the loss of any ale you might have served."

Gytha's eyes grew large, pursing her lips she stared at Dag. "I know you not, think me a foolish woman to wander off into the night with a Jomsviking who lurks in the shadows, the Jarls men might notice I'm gone."

"Do this Gytha, I mean you no harm, meet me and quickly." Dag was not asking and strode away from the woman exiting the tavern through the back door. Almost immediately the stench of open sewers and rotten food assailed his senses, his boots squelched in the fetid mud, 'disgusting oaf!' he thought and relished the opportunity to smack the woman's brother about the head. Dag knew well that were there was the rotten stench of decay there was illness and disease.

The stables he sought out were but a stones throw away, he could smell the manure of the beasts and the grass they ate, he would purchase one or two horses and make haste to the farmstead. A man stood outside the stables puffing on a large pipe, he was not much older than Dag but twice the weight and balding, he raised his eyebrows as the Viking approached.

"I want two, strong and reliable, what have you got?" Dag grunted at the man.

"None for sale. Some men came earlier and bought the last, they come to pick the nags up later." As the fat man spoke wisps of smoke leaked from his mouth, he had scraggly whiskers stained by the tobacco; his greasy skin glistened in the torch burning overhead.

"I can offer you more than they did… what's your price?" Dag jostled his coin pouch.

The man stepped forward and ushered him into the stable, beckoning Dag the man waddled to the rear of the building where grains and tools were piled against a wooden panelled wall. "They were the Jarls men, they paid as little as they could, you seem like a man of his word and so I'll take your coin. When they come back I'll feign stupidity… wait here I heard something!" The man picked up his pace and ran back to the entrance. Dag peered over his shoulder and saw a small figure clutching a leather sack to her chest.

"Wait, she's with me, Gytha come over here." Dag saw the young woman and the man approach; emptying a few gold pieces into his palm he offered them to the horse merchant who greedily swiped them into his grasp. His pipe still wedged between his teeth clicked as he counted his profit.

"Yes yes… take what you want but quickly I do not wish to explain myself with you here!" The sloth waddled away thrusting the gold into his own purse.

"He is dishonest Dag, best we move, often he is in the tavern." Gytha watched as Dag lifted the bar and led two strong beasts into the space between them. Placing the bits between their teeth and throwing a blanket over their backs he handed Gytha the leather straps and led the way into the deserted street.

"Follow me." He whispered. "Did any see you come this way? Other than the merchant? What said your brother?"

"None saw that I know of, my brother scolded me but thinks only of the money you offered, but the horse merchant may be headed to drink his fill at my brothers. He has a loose foolish tongue." Gytha looked into the blackness that had become the night with a worried stare.

Dag nodded and noticed her hair was hanging loosely from her braid on one side. "Did he mistreat you because of my request?"

"Ja but no matter, when you give me the coin for healing I have vowed never to return to him but head north, there's naught left for me here and I can't even say that at least I am protected in my brother's house." Gytha's lips thinned and she looked Dag square in the eye.

"A woman travelling alone is a danger to herself. And the settlements to the north are smaller than here."

"Why say such a thing, what choice have I got?"

"None I suppose." Dag was perplexed with his feelings, he liked this woman despite himself but also had no need for a dependant female, he felt somewhat responsible for her most recent mistreatment. "Come... if your healing powers are worth the money mayhap we will escort you as far north as we plan to travel ourselves."

"How many are you?" Gytha quickened her pace to keep up with Dag and the horses. They walked steadily to the path leading to the edges of the town, it was a walk she had taken few times as the people there did not often call for a healer or visit the dockside taverns.

"Three." He lifted a finger to his lips and smiled. "Keep up!"

Gytha strained in the darkness to see where Dag was leading them, his pace was quick and she grew breathless, she wished he would light a torch but reasoned it was unwise to draw attention to themselves. More than once she cursed when stubbing a toe on an overturned rock and again when she heard the man in front of her snigger. He was handsome, she knew with a bright smile that she guessed had won many a woman over, she had played coy and blushed when he looked at her but she would give nothing away, he was helping her escape. When they had met that afternoon she felt that it would not be the last time they saw one another. It was her insightful qualities that drew her brother's ire and his wife's.

In childhood her mother had sent her often to the Volur women for potions and herbs to treat her ailing father, little worked and her brother became sour and distrustful, but the women took the time to teach Gytha their ways and encourage her sight. Gytha had prayed to the Gods every night that her father would recover and allow her to join the women in their encampment beyond the township. Neither had happened.

Suddenly Gytha felt a shiver creep over her skin, her ears buzzed and flashes of light crossed her eyes. Rubbing her fingers against her eyelids she stalled in her tracks.

"What is it?" Dag turned sensing the horse behind him had stopped.

"I don't know… how far away are we?"

"Paces… here take my arm I'll lead the horses." Dag felt the woman's hand on his shoulder and he guided them into the small steading. Tying the two beasts to the barn post he turned Gytha to the door of the small houses and led her inside.

Drawing a sharp breath Gytha looked past the man who stood to meet them to the form on the pallet behind him. Dropping her hand from Dag's arm she rushed to the woman laying covered in furs. Her skin seemed unnaturally aglow; Gytha sucked in a breath and swung to face the men.

"By the Gods who are you?" Gytha almost shouted.

"What?! Dag who is this?" Ari hissed at his friend.

"Be calm both of you! Ari this is Gytha a healer, Gytha what causes you to act so? Can you heal her?" Dag looked with confusion to Gytha.

Turning back to the woman Gytha placed a hand on her brow, she was in a fever, as she removed her hand a stabbing vision exploded in her mind. She saw the woman with a child, a boy, they were walking across the rainbow bridge into Asgard. Around them the stars fell from Gimli and landed at the child's feet, the woman lifted the boy pointed to a man standing far away in the distance, the man held a long staff and slammed it into the ground. From the root of the staff the ground split in two and wondrous burning light erupted all about them. Gytha drew a breath and staggered back into the chest of Dag. The other man named Ari looked at her with concern.

"What is it?" He asked.

"I must be sure, help me." Gytha lifted the woman's shoulders and wrestled her dress from her shoulders exposing the pale skin beneath.

"What are you doing?" Dag asked incredulously.

"By the Gods she is… what is her name? Tell me." Gytha demanded staring angrily at the two men.

"She is Liv…" Ari spoke quietly. "What is it?"

Gytha stood and folded her arms about her waist struggling to find the words. "She is a protector, her name means life, and she has a branding on her back. Who are you men… did you do this to her?"

Dag raised his hands to Gytha ushering her to sit. Ari turned away, resting his fists on the table he slowly sunk down to the bench and took a seat. Liv stirred slightly on the pallet and the room fell into silence.

# 5.

Jarl Brynjar drummed his fingers on the wooden table impatiently, he had sent three men to Gulafjord in search of the Jomsviking Gorm who had failed to deliver the woman and the boy, two of the Jomsvikings had returned and been sent away unpaid for their dismal efforts.

"Tell me… how much must I pay?" Brynjar growled at his captain. "This woman evades capture again, how does she do it? Does the ring empower her with invisibility?"

"I cannot say Jarl."

"Must I ride out and fetch her myself?" He threw hateful looks at the man before him. "What are you doing about this?"

Holger bit his tongue, he hated the Jarl but could do nothing about it, he felt nothing but irritation for the quest Jarl Brynjar was set upon. It was ridiculous that a man of his standing should covet a legend to the detriment of his men. The Jarl also reneged on his word on many an occasion and Holger could not abide such a character but he was sworn to serve the man by his own foolish consent.

"The Jomsviking were not our own men, there was no way of knowing their true allegiance, it appears the one called Gorm has taken an opportunity. Mayhap we will receive word that he holds the woman and the boy hostage for more money? Perhaps he has killed them and taken the ring, then he is a thief and we will track him down, the three I sent are highly trained…"

"Your words are full of defeat! This Gorm will lose his head; nay he'll suffer a pit of vipers for betraying me so, further from my grasp this wench has become again! In my lands she trod and none could bring her to me?!" Brynjar slammed his fist on the table standing angrily he shoved the heavy oak chair from behind his jaw clenched in fury. "So damned close, by the God's I swear Loki is aiding her at every turn. Trickster, demon, witch!"

Holger watched as the man's eyes bulged, his thick hair tied back from his face showed the veins throbbing in his forehead, and with barely calloused fingers Jarl Brynjar massaged his temples. The Jarl wore the finest tunic's and wore many jewels on his fingers but the shine wore away from all he touched such was his greed and lust for wealth. Holger fought to think of a time when the Jarl had been honourable and just, he was harsh and uncompromising now, and he could not remember when it was the tale had been told of the ring and its rightful heir. It was the talk of old wives and worn out warriors who had seen too much life taken from them, their minds addled with grief and years of regret, his own mother has spoken in such ways before she died and he had hated the wistful look in her eyes when she spoke of seidr and myths.

The Jarls hall was as richly furnished as its owner, it was adorned with wooden carvings in the posts and beams. Large shields and swords hung from the walls and the platform, from which the Jarl sat and feasted with his men, gave judgement and made plans, was swathed in rich tapestries woven by his wife and her women. The Jarl had but one lacking of which he was greatly ashamed, the source of his ire and frustration, he had no children.

Though he had taken two wives and many mistresses none were round with his offspring, his men said nothing but cast glances at one another when time and again the Jarl boasted of his prowess but had produced no evidence, Brynjar himself came from a large family with many a brother who sought to take the seat as Jarl and continue the line. As a result Jarl Brynjar had outcast all his sisters who had proven fertile with strong sons and killed one of his own brothers in what many suspected was a Dagger tainted with poison. Three brothers remained who had all vowed loyalty to Brynjar but they neither trusted him or one another.

Holger himself had a son and a daughter, he knew the Jarl held a bitter resentment of this as he considered his captain of lower ranking and therefore not an equal. It was only because he was sworn to the Jarl that he and his family remained in Srovberget. He had desperately hoped the Jomsviking would have found the woman and put the matter to rest but it seemed they had not been able to live up to their names. The Jarl's own men had been dispatched to

Gulafjord when the two men who had accompanied Gorm ventured a ship had been in the settlements harbour when they had been in pursuit of the woman. Gulafjord was a potential nightmare, from there Gorm might have taken any number of ships and escaped, even if the man had taken the woman and child by foot they would at least have procured horses and the roads to Gulafjord were heavy with those on route to the Thing. Where the Jarl Brynjar should have been preparing to travel to but he shunned it and that would be noticed Holger thought.

"Thank Odin the Jomsviking was not informed of the boy's true identity." The Jarl regained his composure and sat facing Holger once more. "I want you to ride out to Gulafjord and find this Gorm…"

"If I am gone Jarl… there would be none to watch your back." Holger offered dryly.

"None would dare Holger, it is not your presence alone that stops the Daggers plunging into my back, there are men aplenty to stand guard."

"Then you will not attend the Thing in Gulafjord?"

"No!" Brynjar slammed his open palm on the table. "What have you to say about it?"

Holger took a breath. "Your absence will be noticed, we cannot appear weak in front of the other Jarls, and should word reach the King…"

"Once we have the ring and the boy none of that will matter." The words dripped from Brynjar's mouth like pebbles, each one echoing around the dimly lit room as they hit the floor.

With a nod Holger resigned himself to the knowledge that this was a pointless conversation, the Jarl was so deeply entrenched in his belief of the legend that he could see no sense, but another troubling point was presenting itself. Holger had noted over the last six years the frequency with which the Jarls rages had increased, every time he was defeated or outwitted by the woman he appeared in physical pain often rubbing his temple or forehead. On these occasions he would slump into his seat as if the day had been spent training hard with the men and drained of strength.

"Go now." Jarl Brynjar waved a hand in front of his captain and watched as the man turned and strode from the hall. It irked him greatly that Holger felt he had the right to challenge his decision of attending the Thing. If he himself saw it as no dereliction of duty or admittance of loss of power then what was it to Holger he mused? Brynjar stretched his legs from beneath the table and frowned when he noticed a tremor in his left foot.

For some time he had been ignoring the twitching of the limb, soon his hand would follow suit, he would call for the healer and have her prepare a brew. His calls upon her witchcraft were becoming more frequent; he detested the healing women with their secret knowledge and magic. If he had an interest he would have learned their art but he had no time for the darkness of women's souls; they were all alike to him. He had taken two empty vessels for wife and no potion or spell or prayer had provided him with a child from their wombs. He had taken many a mistress and all they were good for was sating his desire, in the end they all wanted one thing; to become the Jarls wife, his only wife.

The tremor in his foot paused for a moment allowing Brynjar to raise himself from his seat and head towards the passageway concealed behind the tapestries hanging behind his seat. The passage was dimly lit as he walked to his chamber, he noted that the servants were conspicuously absent. More than likely they had heard his ranting at Holger and decided to make themselves scarce, 'Wise!' he thought with a grim smile. Reaching the chamber he found his wife was nowhere to be seen, thankful for this he lay down on the fur covered bed and allowed exhaustion to creep over him.

He began to think of the boy, it always started like this for him, the child was always first to enter his thoughts followed soon after by the prize; the ring. Brynjar thought of the day he learned of the legend and the man who had promised him his loyalty; where was that man now he thought? True he had sent messengers, his actions had been swift on the mere hint of a rumoured sighting, but it appeared that he was no closer to locating the woman for himself. Then the suggestion of the Jomsvikings; the idea had not appealed to Brynjar as the mercenaries were costly but that they would catch the woman more swiftly than he had been able to had been appealing. The man had had the one named Gorm in mind for the task such was his skill at tracking; it would appear, Brynjar thought, he was as equally skilled at treachery.

Alarm tickled Byrnjar's pulse causing him to sit up quickly. Could it be, he wondered, that this Gorm and the man were working with one another? For his contact had managed to find a man who had achieved what Brynjar had not; mayhap the old man no longer found him worthy of the prize?

A memory of the old man floated into the Jarls mind; he saw his father with the old man who was much younger then, he saw them pointing to maps drawing plans together. They spoke of battle with other feudal Chief's and the man correctly predicted Brynjar's father's victory in each case. He remembered the tears in the eyes of the man when Brynjar's father breathed his last and it was then that the man told him of the legend and swore his oath to Brynjar.

No, he shook his head, the man would never betray him although in the past he had indeed failed him. True it had been many a year since they had last set eyes upon one another but through messengers they had maintained a level of contact.

At that moment the Jarls wife swept into the room, catching sight of her husbands face she drew a heavily ringed hand to her chest and gasped, she was a fine woman to look upon but had lost her lustre somewhat over the past few years.

"Husband! What ails you?" She took a seat by Brynjar.

"My head aches, my limbs are weary... where have you been? Where are the servants?" He snapped at her.

Meekly the woman looked at the floor and stood, turning she walked to the door and closed it. Brynjar only now noticed that her eyes were rimmed with redness and her cheeks stained with tears. "Your brother's wife... her labour was early, neither survived. The servants are preparing for her burial."

"No word reached my ears on this."

"You have been so busy Brynjar, I could not bother you with this news, and your brother does not know himself."

A wry smile spread across Brynjar's lips. "You have done well wife, tis my duty to tell him, ensure two of my men escort him here before he arrives home."

"Brynjar… is that wise?"

"You question me?" He snapped, wildly throwing a terse look in her direction he rose to his feet but stumbled towards his wife instead of walking. "Woman fetch the healer now!" He roared at her.

Brynjar's wife quickly walked to the doorway but as she passed Brynjar's form resting his hands on the framework of the bed the Jarl grasped her arm and squeezed tightly. "Do not think to question me again!" He growled in her ear. "No-one speaks to Inge before I, understand Solveig?"

Shaking with pain Solvieg nodded, barely able to bring herself to look at her husband. Warily she locked eyes with him and expected his free hand to deliver a blow, but it did not come, breathing deeply she felt his grip weaken and pulling free Solvieg ran from the room in search of the healer.

Tears sprung in her eyes as she ran, her heart lurched from the pain of her brother-in-laws loss and the awful vengeance her husband had in mind, she wondered how much more she would have to take from the wrathful Brynjar. It was true that Inge was not in Srovberget he was on an errand of mercy in her name for Solvieg had asked Inge to aid her in escape from Brynjar. She had reasoned that of all the men to aid her Inge would have been the least suspected when the Jarl would have discovered her gone. Inge was the youngest of his brothers and the least challenging to Brynjar by his own admission. Brynjar tolerated Inge in the hall on occasion and gloried that his younger sibling had never made an attempt on his life or was likely to. Brynjar did not hold Inge in esteem of any kind for the man was a cripple and yet he still fathered children much to Solvieg's joy and Brynjar's annoyance.

Solvieg had given Inge the last of her mothers jewellery to pay for passage to the far east of the kingdom where her remaining family would hide her from the Jarl, in truth Solvieg suspected that Brynjar would be enraged but not enough to send his men out into the world looking for her at least not when he was so obsessed with the woman and the child. But now her plans were up in smoke, Inge would return to a house of death, Brynjar would deliver the terrible news with malice. Such would be Inge's grief that Solvieg could no longer ask or rely upon his help to flee.

For a maddening fraction of a moment Solvieg stopped in her tracks and considered a terrible thought. The healer held no love for Jarl Brynjar, he often maligned her until he was in need of her craft, would she help Solvieg? Looking at the rings on her fingers she wondered which one might offer enough coin and not be missed by the Jarl if she were to offer it in payment to the healer for poison. But as soon as Solvieg considered the possibility she shuddered and continued with her task, she could no more kill Brynjar than allow him to deliver the awful news to Inge.

On this she knew she would defy her husband, she would somehow get word to her husband's brother and prepare him as best she could, and mayhap if Brynjar's wrath was so great as to deliver her the beating that might end her life so be it.

# 6.

Though Gytha had argued against moving Liv, when she was so weak, the men would not consider the possibility of being caught by the Jarls men. The three hunters were already in Gulafjord and only a short distance away was enough to set Ari's mind; they had to move and quickly.

"But to where?" Gytha panicked. They had still not fully explained who they were and what they were doing with the woman, Gytha felt sure that the one called Ari had not beaten her such was the concern in his eyes when she examined her body.

"Giffni... the hot spring cave, our village is not far from there and we will be safe for a few days." Ari spoke quickly as he strapped his mantle across his shoulders and then the leather strap of his sword belt across his back. "Dag did you..."

Dag raised a hand and spoke swiftly. "A few hours ride we will reach a fishing hamlet, there a small boat awaits but there will be no room for the horses aboard. Mayhap we leave them in payment to the villagers?"

"It is not enough that you are Jomsvikings?" Gytha quizzed but took a breath as both men threw her fiery looks.

"People talk Gytha, buying silence is necessary. Gather your things." Dag spoke with military command. It shocked Gytha to see his easy going and humorous nature disappear to be replaced by a soldier. Part of her admired his ability to switch between the different aspects of his personality but she also felt a fear, more so from the silent man called Ari who dark stare and grim expression told her the gravity of the situation.

"Who is the Jarl that seeks her... why?" Gytha lifted her leather bag throwing the strap over her shoulder, moving to Liv she pulled her worn clothing about the woman more tightly.

"Gytha if you come with us it will be a hard journey and dangerous, can you give us what Liv needs..." Ari spoke with no emotion.

"I'm coming! You can't leave me here Dag! My brother… all I need is passage north and I will not leave her she is watched over by the Gods!"

Both men stood startled by the outburst from the woman. Dag's eyes flickered with interest that the small soft form of the woman had taken on a straight erect line, her shoulders squared and her jaw set, she was not what he had thought. "Come then but no more questions until we have time to speak of it."

Ari looked at Dag and shook his head; his friend shrugged his shoulders and guided Gytha to the horses tied outside. Lifting Liv from the pallet Ari carried her to Grani and set her gently upon his back. Climbing astride he took a rope and tied it about his waist and that of Liv's; he would not risk her falling from the horses back and injuring herself further. Throughout this Liv did not stir nor flutter an eyelash. Ari swallowed dryly wondering how long it would take her to come round. The springs at Giffni were a refuge they had found when they were young and he hoped that she would not be too alarmed when she awoke to discover how close to their old settlement they would be.

It was a mystery to Ari why Liv did not want to return to their home. True she had lived there in thrall status but he had taken an oath with her and his father had not argued the matter when Ari told him he was to wed her. She would have been freed from servitude and have his protection against all who would seek to harm her or command her. Perhaps she was afraid of what the people might have to say at her hasty departure, they thought she was a runaway slave, perhaps she feared punishment. It would not happen thought Ari, his father was the brother of the Chieftain and Ove was not a vengeful man. In fact all had been perturbed by her disappearance and when Harvardr had explained it was due to her wandering bloodline they accepted she had never been one of their own. Her people were nomadic; at least her father had been, Liv's mother had been pregnant with her when she had washed ashore near their settlement. The woman had been near death but held on long enough to birth her daughter. It was when they came to cleanse and prepare the body for burial, they discovered the thrall collar about her neck she had kept concealed under her cloak. Upon the discovery Ove gave Liv to the thrall women to raise instead of casting her out to the elements.

Grani snorted as the fresh night air tickled his nostrils, Ari guided him to join Dag and Gytha where they sat on horseback with hunted stares. Nodding to Dag Ari dug his heels into Grani's side and the horse sprung into a gallop.

The three rode hard for hours stopping only once to allow Ari and Gytha a moment to check on Liv's condition. Her eyes rolled back in her head and she groaned slightly when Gytha pushed her loose hair away from her ear to check for fresh blood. Satisfied that the bleeding had stopped, they pushed onwards.

The hamlet was comprised of a few fishing huts adjacent to the beach. Nets hung from trestles' and racks for drying herring perched beside each household. The air held a briny odour. A faint smell of smoke hung in the air at this late hour Ari guessed that the inhabitants were sleeping for not a soul stirred from a doorway as they approached. Dag jumped down from his horse crossing the shore and rapping his knuckles against the door of a lean-to shack. Gruffly a small figure appeared rubbing his face and swearing under his breath.

Gytha stared as the large Viking prodded the bad tempered old man in the chest; the man raised his hands and disappeared back inside the shack before reappearing with his cloak. Grunting at the group he beckoned them to follow. Gytha felt oddly aware that no-one else had stuck their noses out of their dwellings and by now she was sure they would know strangers had come into their hamlet. Could it be the houses were deserted and this man was the keeper of the land? Ari reading her thoughts turned and whispered reassuringly.

"Most likely he remains while all else travel to the Thing in Gulafjord. These people are poor by the looks of it, there is coin to be made whilst so many are travelling."

Gytha nodded and jumped down from her horse making to follow Dag and the old man. Ari led Grani by the reins while Liv's body slumped forward on the horses back. Slowly they walked around a grassy mound on the shoreline and found a small boat dragged onto the shingle.

"It will do." Said Dag clearly irritated.

"And the nags?" The old man grunted, Gytha could see he was missing many teeth and his sour breath reached her nose.

"Not a chance. Where is your son? This isn't the boat he showed me; does he hide from the beating that's due?" Dag bore down on the man grinning but without humour.

"He sleeps… some men from the township beat him senseless, he followed you to the docks talking about going Viking… what does a fisherman's son want with that?!" The man stepped back and spat into the sand.

"Get him." Said Ari.

The fisherman hastily took the path along which they had come moments later he dragged a youth behind him who face was a myriad of cuts and bruises. Dag stood tall and crossed his arms over his chest, Ari placed a hand on the strap of his belt, the Jomsvikings glared down at the boy before looking at one another and nodding.

"I am not happy, my friend here less happy about this than I. What say you?" Dag spoke slowly.

Gytha felt an anger rise in her chest, how could they be so unkind when the boy was clearly afraid, she saw the boy's eyes widen and his whole body began to tremble.

"Please Master Dag! I made a mistake we did have a larger vessel, but I lost it in a game of dice." He scratched absently at the back of his head before casting his look downwards. "I will take a beating…"

"Gambling? Who with?"

"Viking traders."

"Which ship?" Dag cocked his head in query.

"One I tried to join but they laughed at me, cheated me in dice and beat me until I ran."

"You wanted to become a Viking?" Dag smiled, no wonder they had used the boy in jest he looked pathetic even now with his tufted hair sticking up and his clothes shapeless and hanging from his thin shoulders, but still to beat the lad was cruel.

"Like you." The boy shot a sideways glance at Dag before looking at Gytha and blushing.

Dag looked at Ari and shook his head. The boy was too slight and had clearly never been in the training fields. He looked malnourished and he bruises didn't help to impress any kind of masculinity about him.

"Well boy mayhap you can still prove your worth? How do you ride?" Ari asked.

"Uh… well…" The boy looked between the two men nervously.

"Your father can manage without you for some days?" Dag quizzed.

The old man nodded quickly and placed a hand on the boy's shoulder. "Ja…"

"Then you will take our horses to Giffni, we will meet you on the edge of the great lake where the cliffs jut out into the fjord. Take the back roads, avoid anyone at all costs, you would be an easy target, one boy with three beasts. We need these horses and you need to prove yourself." Ari scrutinised the boy, his eyes hot with pride at the task that Jomsvikings had given him, he felt reluctant to let the boy become overly excited and stepped closer to him with a grave look in his eyes. "Do not get caught."

The old man choked erupting into a fit of coughing; his son turned and patted him on the back all the while feeling the eyes of the two large men watching him, gulping the boy nodded nervously. "I can do that… I'll disguise the horses muddy them so they look old and worthless, I'll dress in rags and an old cloak so any I meet think me sick, they would be sure to avoid me."

"Cunning… I like it!" Dag grinned before gesturing to the old man and boy to set about their business.

In the dark before the breaking of the new morning sun Ari and Dag dragged the boat down to the water's edge. They had two oars each and at first would row together. Gytha gathered her belongings from the back of her steed and lingered by Grani and Liv until Ari returned to carry Liv and the packs from horses saddle to the boat. Gytha noted a tinge of sadness about the man when he handed over Grani's reins to the boy; she wondered about this sombre man, he appeared not at all like the Vikings that had frequented her brother's tavern. Not that Dag was altogether what she expected either.

True she had toyed with the notion of letting him have his way when first they met at the harbour. But much had changed since then, the notion had let form a foolhardy plot whereby Dag would beat her brother senseless but it had not come to fruition and for this she was glad. Violence was a natural fact of life but Gytha sought to heal and never inflict wounds upon any person herself.

She watched Dag silently, she guessed he was a rogue but something else told her there was more to the man for did mercenaries and cut-throats have friends and did they try to bring healers to women who were secretly guardians? She thought not. And what of this man Ari? He obviously cared for the woman; this was an attribute that soldiers rarely indulged in if the men of the drinking house were anything to go by. The men were a contradiction to their Jomsviking status she mused.

Gytha held her leather bag to her chest, she reminded herself of one thing, what would happen when they reached their destination, they were Jomsvikings after all and she knew not what their mission was and furthermore it appeared they were not entirely informed of the unconscious woman.

Dag waved Gytha to come forward, stepping into the boat she slid into the spot beside Liv checking her temperature and the rapidity of the throbbing pulse in her neck, she desperately wanted Liv to awaken.

"I will have one last word with them." Dag spoke to Ari.

Ari nodded and started to load their weapons, swords, axes and Daggers. Adding to that he had two skins of drinking water and a cloth sack filled with flat bread dried fish and meat. All the while he darted his gaze here and there about the shore and the hamlet of small huts. The darkness was silent, no beating of hooves not the shouts of men betrayed themselves, and all was still.

"I can see the look of concern on your face Gytha... there is naught to fear from us."

"Thank you, for taking me with you, for as long as you will."

"There may be danger ahead we cannot guarantee your safety... should you have to run then do so." Ari narrowed his eyes as he watched the young woman stroke the side of Liv's face.

"How well do you know her?" Gytha whispered.

Ari straightened his back, climbing into the boat he sat on a small plank at the first set of oars from the prow, resting his elbow on his knees he sighed heavily. "Very well... once."

"Once?" Gytha cocked an eyebrow. "You were parted?"

"Ja many years ago, before I became a Jomsviking."

"So you are not the boy's father?" Gytha instantly winced as she saw the man's face harden as he closed eyes; he seemed to be in pain she thought.

"How do you know about the boy?"

"I saw it when I touched her."

"Saw it?" Ari stared hard at the woman. She was smaller than Liv in height, her hair was thick and blonde, and her eyes were a pale hue. Her youthful frame still soft and lithe. He realised what interest Dag had in her but this new idea that she had more knowledge than the workings of herbs and spells bothered him. "You are Volur?"

"Nay, though I spent much time with a settlement of Volur as a child, sometimes I see things but they are like dreams... until I touched her."

"Liv, you can use her name, she would like it. Being on the run you don't use your real name often."

"Liv..." Gytha smiled at the sleeping form. "There are many men who distrust women like me."

"And women who feel the same about a Viking." Ari rubbed the back of his neck with a tired hand. "You have naught to fear from us."

"That's twice you have said that, I believe you, I'll do what I can to help. Her heart is heavy, it keeps her sleeping, her mind needs time to set the present to right. I think she fears for the boy."

"Feared perhaps…"

"What?" Gytha shot a glance at Ari who was looking towards the dark figure approaching them. Dag was wading through the calf deep water and the boat rocked slightly in his wake.

Ari lifted the oars staring as his friend. "The boy is dead."

Dag climbed into the boat and took the oars in front of Ari, together they pulled and the little boat pushed off into the open water. Steadily the men made a great distance before the sun began to rise. All the while Gytha's focus remained with the woman beside her.

'Why did you lie to him?' She wondered.

Feeling drained and tired Gytha closed her eyes and listened to the men as they spoke of direction and how long it would take to reach Giffni, she knew not where that was though the men had mentioned many days travel. They muttered on and Gytha kept her eyes closed until Ari said Smalsahorn, in a flash she was wide eyed and staring at the two men who brows were beaded with sweat and their tunics rolled at the sleeves.

"Smols?!" Gytha breathed.

"Dag caught her eye and grinned with a full set of teeth. "Ja Gytha we sail to Smols! You will see Ari's mountain Smalsarhorn where the God's stand and watch over Midgard!"

"Hah, I've climbed Smalsarhorn and I found no God's!" Ari chuckled without breaking into a full smile behind his friend all the while pulling on the oars.

"Your gloom scared them away!" Dag laughed heartily but suddenly stopped when Ari flicked water with the blade of his oar and soaked Dag to the skin.

At once all three broke into a reverie of laughter, tears streaming from their eyes, struggling to regain their breath. The men paused and pulled their oars into the boat.

"You have heard of my mountain?" Ari asked Gytha as he passed a skin of water to the dripping Dag.

"Ja… I dreamt of it! I saw someone standing at the edge of its summit but never have I seen that person since. I thought mayhap it was a vision and I cannot deny that now!" Gytha smiled warmly.

"Visions?" Dag stretched his aching arms. "The woman keeps producing interesting talents."

"Indeed." Ari nodded at Gytha and watched as she blushed when she stared then to Dag. Ari assumed Dag was winking or smiling at the young maid who was fair taken with him. 'Just what we need.' Thought Ari, 'A healer, vision's, and a fair face too... Dag is hopeless!' But Ari found himself warmed at the thought his friends roving eye had finally fallen on one so deserving. If only it had happened in a more peaceful time when they were not pursued or sheltering under the cloud of peril.

# 7.

The boy looked at the horses and attempted a quick calculation in his head on how long it would take him to reach Giffni, he reasoned the animals were strong and healthy, he knew he was light of weight and could ride the back of a different horse to let the others rest.

A week he thought, 'It will take a week maybe less if I do not stop often?' The Jomsviking Dag had suggested mere days but the boy figured they would give him some lenience. After all he was delivering them their beasts and they could not travel far without them, even with his father's small boat they would be restricted to the seas and unable to cross land.

As he gathered his sack filled with dried fish, unleavened bread and a skin of water, he mused at what the men were up to. With two women, one being unconscious and the other a rumoured healer, with their need to leave the area of Gulen swiftly he paused to think that perhaps he was involving himself in something more than he could handle.

"Odin's eye Thorik! This was what you wanted, adventure!" Thorik chastised himself in the smoky darkness of his father's hut rummaging through the threadbare cloaks and hoods he would use for his disguise. "Finally a way out of this hovel!"

"Hovel?!" Thorik's father cuffed the boy about the ear and watched with disdain as the boy winced at the blow throwing his father a dirty look. "Ja a hovel indeed! Go on your adventure, see the lands, but return the wiser for it!"

"Sorry father." Thorik grumbled not meaning a word of it. "I won't be gone long and the rest will be back from the Thing before you know it… there won't be time to miss me."

"Miss you?" The old man repeated much to Thorik's dismay. He hated that the old man made a habit of this when they spoke. "I need help to fish not sit and bemoan the loss of our talks at the fireside!"

"Well I won't miss either… till I return." Thorik grumbled huffily.

The old man watched his son gather the cloaks under his arm with the sack and stride out of the hut. His small frame seemed overburdened by his load but it was nothing like what he was about to face. Taking a stool the man sat beside the smouldering fire and roughly rubbed his eyes with his sea hardened hands. 'Why is he so wilful?' He thought.

It was true that Thorik had always sought out trouble and more often than not it had not been a hard task. He fought with the other children, he swam too far in the sea pushed the smaller vessels too hard, approached any stranger who happened to be passing by. When they traded in Gulen Thorik would always wander off and ultimately end up at the harbour side, he appeared drawn to the wildest and roughest of men, where his appetite for excitement was always sated. Often the old man caught Thorik ogling the ships with keen interest or quizzing a grizzly crewman for tales of his conquests; the more gruesome the better.

But Thorik was naught but mild amusement to these types of men and always the boy returned sullenly to his home. He dreamt of adventure and battle dressed in the garb of a Viking warrior, claiming treasure and the respect of those he would one day command, it was all foolish dreams he thought Thorik would never see. But now, however, he had realised his ambition. Yes it had taken a beating and a dent to his pride to achieve it but now Thorik was on his journey.

"Where will this lead?" The old man sighed wearily.

He feared for the boy, perhaps if he had taken a stronger hand with him none of this would have occurred, mayhap the Norn's had woven it this way with their threads of fate. But the boy was thin and looked frail, his father knew he could haul in a net as well as he could but what about fighting and defending himself, he never seemed to gain weight or look healthy such was his waxen skin and dark circles about his eyes. He knew his son slept fitfully and this contributed to his appearance since he had not recovered from his mother's death. In reality the hamlet still mourned her loss but it was the way of the world. It was the way of men in Midgard to suffer so. Not every death had meaning and not every death had dignity. It would be a lucky thing to pass into the afterlife in your sleep he mused.

Warily the old man stood and shuffled to the doorway. He saw his son jump astride the horse the second Jomsviking had ridden, the other two beasts were tethered with rope to one another forming a chain, with a nudge of his heel the horse broke into a trot and the party set off. Thorik did not look back upon his father's home and the old man prayed that the men were honourable and the Gods would favour his son on this task.

Thorik felt his heart beat in his chest, he imagined himself a strong man not to be trifled with, and he sat proudly on Grani's back feeling the strong muscles of the horse as it walked. He resisted the temptation to urge it into a gallop just yet; he would wait until his father's hut was far from view. The morning air was alive with the breath of the sea wind upon his face. Drawing in a deep breath Thorik smiled to himself, he thought of the danger ahead and how he would defeat it, fingering the short sword he had pilfered from a man on the docks some many months ago he felt a surge of excitement that he might have to use it.

"I won't go looking for danger Grani fear not!" He stroked the horse's mane and it snorted at him. Sticking out his bottom lip Thorik wondered if even the animal thought him incapable. "You know Grani they trusted me with your delivery so I'd be kinder to your master!"

The horse shook its mane, without taking a command from Thorik it made its way from the main road to a less well used path leading to rolling fields littered with large boulders, the two beasts attached to them continued without question.

"Do you know where we are headed Grani?" Thorik questioned but the horse remained silent. Shrugging Thorik loosened his grip on the reins and relaxed a little, the horse had taken the path he himself had chosen so it was a wise beast he reasoned, he was in good company.

By the afternoon Thorik had ridden the horses hard and covered much ground. Reaching a small stream he jumped from Grani's back and let them drink. The rest was welcome as he chewed slowly on the dried fish watching the horses eat the wild grasses. The land surrounding them was entirely empty of life, neither wild deer nor boar was to be seen and he had hardly noticed a bird in the sky, it seemed an odd place and Thorik wondered if this was why no settlement had been laid. It was a windswept place littered with rocks and so would have been poor farmland; this was more likely the reason than ideas from his wild imagination.

Gathering the horses he tied Grani to the rear and jumped upon the horse Dag had ridden. It was as sturdy as Grani but the boy favoured the other horse, not wanting to offend the animal he stroked its mane before swiftly kicking its sides into motion, it didn't seem to possess the character of the other beast. As they rode Thorik felt the hours pass in mere moments such was his joy at accomplishing a full day's ride without mishap. When at last he knew he had to stop and make camp he resisted the notion of a fire and instead huddled against the safety of a large boulder allowing tiredness to give him some sleep. Often he jerked awake throughout the night each time rising to check the tethers on the horses, always they were secure, and when at last he could stand it no longer he allowed the bright moonlight that shone down upon them to light their path. Once or twice he felt himself nodding off on horseback but finally as the new dawn arose he snapped awake and surveyed his route.

Still the land was strewn with rock and wild long grasses. But in the distance Thorik could see the line of the coast and the sea air filtered its way to his nose. He allowed Grani to once again take charge and they made their way to the shingle beach. As they approached Thorik saw that the beach stretched for miles, he took the chance and broke the horses into a gallop, there was no sign of boats or huts in fact no sign of human life at all. The sting of the morning air watered his eyes and the salt matted his short tousled tufts of hair. Again the surging feeling of pride rose in his chest and he laughed into the wind, Grani was swift and graceful beneath him.

"You are Odin's horse!" Laughed Thorik.

When they had covered a few miles and the horses slowed to ease their limbs and lungs from the ride Thorik allowed them a moment's rest. Pulling them to a spring trickling onto the stones of the shore he let the horses drink. A wild thought occurred to Thorik, throwing off his cloak he grabbed the short sword from his belt.

Lifting his right arm he swung the blade around his head, thrusting and jabbing at the invisible assailants surrounding him and cutting each one of his attackers down as they swung their axes and long swords at him. Deftly Thorik leapt and ducked each blow, a war cry erupted from his lips and Thorik stood proudly. Looking at the ground he frowned as his footsteps had done nothing but create a mess on the sand. He remembered the sparring of the Viking men from the ship when they practised and their steps had seemed so sure as if in a dance; his own markings in the sand were nothing like that. Those men had been twice his height and weight with larger heavier weapons; Thorik's light frame and meagre weapon betrayed his inexperience and fitness as his chest heaved and his brow slicked with sweat. His tufted hair ruffled in the breeze and grim determination set on his face.

Though his arms ached Thorik lifted the blade once more, again and again he swung the blade slashing and slicing through the air, looking at the steps he took his gaze fell to his feet as he tried to make sure footings in the sand. All of a sudden the ground fell from beneath his feet and his body flew through the air, then the beach rose up to meet him and grit filled his nose and mouth, his chest heaved and his stomach lurched as the air was knocked from his body. Rolling onto his side Thorik spat the grit from his mouth and saw that he had tripped over an upturned stone, the horse Grani looked at him with his large unimpressed eyes before turning back to the stream, feeling ashamed and ridiculous Thorik pulled himself together and strode over to the horses.

Gathering their reins he tugged them into a slow walk back along the shore. At least he could advance upon his destination if he could not improve his sword skills. Thorik felt a dark mood descend over him and thought that at least there had been no-one present to witness his foolishness. As he trudged along the wet sand littered with pebbles smoothed by the continuous turmoil of the seas he wondered if the men would reward him for completing his task, he realised that he still had many days travel ahead of him and decided to take the opportunity each day while the horses rested to practice his skills, there still might be some chance he would become a Viking.

It was not an unrealistic dream for a boy to have and Thorik felt sure that given the proper training he would grow into a strong warrior, it was not a possibility for him that he would remain this skinny wretch of a lad forever, for his father although a small man was broad enough and his uncles too were strong men. His mother had been a woman of slender build but Thorik shook the idea aside that he resembled a woman in any way. He would be strong, he would be fierce, but as he thought this a grumbling began in his stomach and he realised he had to eat. Instead of stopping Thorik took a wedge of bread from his bag and chewed on it as he walked. If he came upon a stream he might fish for fresh catch instead of the dried meat he carried with him. He would forage for wild roots and greenery to bulk up his meals and he knew he must sleep with more effort in the evening. All these things he would do and felt sure they would make a difference when next he would meet the Jomsviking men.

The beach took many hours to walk but the weather stayed on Thorik's side until the early evening. When the skies began to gather grey threatening clouds the boy resigned himself to finding shelter and waiting out the rain that was promised on the air. Thorik thanked the Gods when at last he found a large crop of rocks nestled between the beach and grassy mounds; there he found a worn patch of ground where some goat herder had taken refuge with his beasts. There were the remains of a long dead fire scorched on the flat earth, Thorik tied the horses together on a post protruding from the ground and took a few moments to survey the area. There were no signs of the previous occupants of the shelter, breathing a sign of relief he started to gather dried wood thrown up from the shore and grass to start a fire, when he returned Grani looked at him with his large eyes.

Patting the horse on his nose Thorik set about building his fire and humming a sea song he had one heard a man on the harbour sing. He remembered the words had something to do with the sea God Aegir protecting them from a terrible storm that battered their vessel. Then Thor rippled a great thunder across the skies before Odin slammed his staff into the high sea cliff's and bolts of lightening erupted from the earth. There were also words of sea maidens as beautiful as Frigg and Freya tempting the sailors into their doom. But Thorik thought nothing of women at his age or found them remotely interesting and neither with all his days at sea had he seen these temptresses from the deep.

Striking his flint the bundle of grass smouldered as a small flame flickered into life, sitting back from his kneeling position Thorik slapped his thigh in triumph and began to build the burning mound, the sea air picked up a little pace but the breeze filtered past the little grotto of the boy and his charges. Dusk was beginning to approach and Thorik thought it best to eat and drink before resting his eyes, he would sleep for a few hours and see how the weather faired. If the night prevented them from travelling he would not be silly enough to try and drag three horses through the wind and rain in the darkness; without a bright clear moon or stars to light the night sky he could easily become lost or walk in circles. Though he knew that keeping the sea to his left would prevent such a thing. Still one of the beasts might become lame and how would he explain that to the men?

Thorik pulled his cloak about his shoulders and chewed hungrily feeling sleep beginning to burn his eyes and limbs with weariness. Untying his sword he propped it beside his leather bag, laying back on the ground he rested his head upon it waiting for a wonderful dream of fighting and adventure.

On the beach three men on foot pulled their horses alongside them as they read the tracks in the sand. The leader was tired and his brow furrowed, the other three were silent in his presence such had been his anger when discovering them eating and drinking in the tavern, he had been mightily angry. His ire was stoked even further when the fat squat horse merchant had arrived in the tavern apologising that since the Jarl's men had not come to claim the horses he had to let two of them go to the next purchaser.

Holger had sent one of the group back to the Jarl with a message informing him that a Jomsviking had been spotted in Gulafjord. Holger had a trail and meant to track the man along the coast, there had been no trail in the township itself and Holger reckoned the man would stand out so perhaps he had taken lodging on the outskirts to avoid detection. The township was bustling, it heaved with travellers and their wares, but somehow they had found the wattle and daub steading where they clearly could see hoof prints in the earth.

The fisherman had been easy to press into talking, he revealed quickly that two Jomsvikings had been and taken a boat from him. He also hurriedly said that his son had been given the task of delivering their horses that he was intent on joining them and had already set off on the journey. Holger was but a day behind and intended to push his men as hard as it would take to catch up with the boy. It had not taken long but Holger had to admit the young lad was not slothful, many youths would have become distracted or taken the opportunity to lengthen their task by dalliance but it was not so with this lad.

The thought occurred to Holger that the Jomsviking men had either struck a cold fear into the boy or impressed the return of their horses with urgency. Either way it meant little to Holger, what really bothered him was that he could not persuade the fisherman to reveal who else travelled with the men, what their names were and their destination.

Holger also felt uneasy that now there were two of these men for him to contend with, he had not known this figuring that the original group of three had been all that were deployed, however he had his own men and all he had to do was deliver the woman to the Jarl.

A gust of wind stirred about the men and a whiff of smoke filtered its way to Holger's nose. Lifting his head he squinted along the line of grassy dunes and waved to the two men behind him. Steadily making their way to the dunes Holger halted and handed the reins of his horse to one of the men. Slowly he found a beaten path in the growing darkness and the smell of fire and animals grew stronger.

Thorik started suddenly from his slumber, one of the horses was whinnying, Grani lifted a front hoof slamming it onto the ground and shaking his mane. The boy rose up on his elbows and wiped the sleep from his eyes, the fire had burned to embers, a chill crept over Thorik's skin. Fingering the blade at the head of his bag he tugged but the weapon could not be moved.

Thorik twisted and darted a look to the sword upon it was a large leather boot. Sharply the boy sprang to his knees and shuffled backwards towards the stamping Grani.

"So boy... we have you at last." The man growled.

The firelight cast a demonic look over the man's features causing Thorik to gasp. He saw a huge bulk of a man with thick fiery hair tied at the back of his head, his eyes were as dark pools of anger, his short neat beard as red as his mane almost seemed to snarl at him. He wore fine clothes that were travel weary but this man was rich or important the boy thought. In his right hand the man extended his long sword that too appeared to glint with evil intent in the glow of the embers. Thorik swallowed and felt fear but also ashamed that he had not come closer to completing his task before failure.

# 8.

The two men by the fireside held their sides as laughter exploded from their chests. The source of their amusement was the young boy Thorik who sat bound at the wrists and ankles with rope. Holger was deeply unamused, the men had no place guffawing at the youth when he had successfully managed to get this far and they were the Jarl's men. He resisted the urge to strike them with an open hand across the face if for nothing else than to silence them.

"A Jomsviking!" The younger of the men pointed at the boy. "You!"

"Hah! My wife would better make a soldier than you!" The other wiped tears from his grimy face.

Thorik turned away from the men with a distant look in his eyes. Holger guessed that he had often been on the wrong side of a jest and knew well to hold his tongue. Staring hard at the ground Thorik resisted the urge to cry with rage. The boy was dumbfounded by the turn of events; how could it be he was followed? He had been careful he thought; how would he ever explain his foolishness should he meet with the Jomsviking men?

Chastising his loose tongue he swallowed and tasted the copper of his own blood still salty in his mouth. It had only taken a few back handed blows before he submitted to the fierce looking men before he mumbled a response admitting that these were their horses. The red haired warrior had shouted at the men to cease and had revealed his father had already told them of his desire to join the Jomsvikings and become one of them himself. The amusement it brought the other men grated on Thorik, he realised that their reactions confirmed the nagging doubts he had pushed far into the recesses of his mind.

He would never become a Viking or a warrior and least of all a Jomsviking. He was too small too slight and sickly of appearance. He would never grow into a strong sword wielding man. If he carried any luck bestowed by Aegir, the God of the sea, his fate would see him return to his father and fish until death saw fit to take him. His father. Thorik clenched his jaw that his own father could give him away so easily; what hope did he have when his own kin betrayed him he wondered.

Suddenly the leader stood and ordered the men to survey the beach and the dunes surrounding them, the men grumbled before standing and shuffling off into the darkness. The man took a seat by the fire, Thorik felt his eyes boring holes into his skin, turning his head ever so slightly Thorik caught his gaze before looking away to Grani.

"Tis a fine animal… yours?" Holger nodded to the grey stallion.

"Nei."

"None of these are yours?"

"Nei."

"What do you own?"

"Nothing now." Thorik shrugged his shoulders and felt the tight rope bite into his skin.

Holger looked at the boy for a moment. Aside from his small stature and wiry frame there was not so much to laugh about. His hair gave him an innocent but elfish look matched by his sharp eyes, he had made it this far on his own merit. "How old are you?"

"Twelve winters…" Thorik mumbled.

"What training have you had then that makes you worthy to join the Jomsvikings?"

"None… but…"

"You know to gain entry you have to fight a man, more often than not they are seasoned warriors."

"No, ja, I mean three more winters and I'd be better than now…"

"Mayhap you thought these men would train you, turn you into a man? Why not go a Viking then? Surely you have sea legs?" Holger smirked at his own joke but secretly felt appalled that his men had been so rough handed with the boy. He was nothing but a foolish young child not yet ready for the world of men and not too far removed from the fantasies of children. He thought of his own son and how angry he would have been if he discovered another had beat him; he did not think this boys father would care much.

"Tis not wrong to wish for more of a life." Thorik spat the words and instantly regretted the venom he shot at the man when his face grew tight with anger. Standing he walked over to him looming above his face.

"Boy's like you have two choices. One; you accept your fate and hope to live well enough. Two; you become a trickster, filled with cunning and guile, a thief a spinner of tales, at best mayhap a trader... the sharpness of your tongue lets me think the latter. What adventures would the God's afford on one with such limited abilities?" Holger's dark stare bore down on Thorik threatening to crush him.

"I..." He swallowed. "I got this far..."

"Hmph." Holger stood and strode back to the meagre fire throwing a handful of driftwood upon it. "So even you have no idea what your future holds? All men must know this, all men must have a plan, for a man is nothing without a destiny." But even as he spoke Holger heard Jarl Brynjar's voice and not his own.

Turning back to the boy Holger pulled a Dagger from his boot, grabbing Thorik's wrists he cut through the rope binding his hands and then his feet. Releasing him from his bonds he grabbed his shoulder and dragged him to the fire.

"Sit." Holger commanded.

Thorik stared at the large man with wide eyes. He stood as tall as the men he had failed, his shoulders broad and even beneath his tunic and cloak the strength of his body was evident, Holger was dangerous Thorik thought. Biting his lip he looked at the man's face and was surprised to see it was not a look of anger but weariness that fixed his features. The man was formidable with his long firey hair, his eyes were a rich blue to match his cloak and his nose though sharp had at one point been broken. His face bore the whiskers of days traveling without shaving and this gave him a more rugged look. Thorik guessed he was a seasoned guard of his Jarl and his face bore the lines of an older man.

"Boy do you know aught of the Jomsviking way? Other than battling? Tis a harsh life, some men would think it harder than most, you would most likely die trying to enter their order." Holger lowered to the fire resting his elbow on one knee and prodded the flames with a dry stick.

"I know they are respected and feared." Thorik spoke with a dry throat. "I only want to be like them."

"Hmm, many do, many young like you and other men too but not all who seek the confines of their keep are honourable."

"Did you hurt my father?"

"No." Holger looked directly into the boy's pale eyes.

"But he told you…"

"Pain is not always necessary to retrieve what you need."

"You threatened him?"

"Ja."

"But he is well?"

Holger lifted the stick and snapped it in his large hand tossing the remnants aside he sighed. "He is."

"The other men didn't threaten him." Thorik knew that wasn't strictly true.

"Well then they must be honourable." A muscle began to twitch in Holger's jaw. Thorik saw it and swallowed nervously realising his tongue had gotten him into deep water once more.

"Please let me go, I'll only take the grey, I'll return to my father."

"No."

"Please…"

"If I let you go the last place you would go is to your father. Do you think me mad or foolish? A boy like you would set off for my quarry and warn them!" Holger laughed releasing one bronze brooch on his cloak and pulling it from his shoulders.

Seeing that he had little chance of release Thorik realised that escape was next to impossible. He stared again at Grani whose large black eyes glittered hypnotically in the light from the fire and the torches the men had lit. A thought occurred to Thorik.

"How come you know so much of the Jomsvikings?" He asked.

"I knew one." Holger thought painfully of his brother. He had enlisted upon the death of their father, the Jarl had chosen Holger to join the ranks of his men but refused entry to Holger's brother. The man had had little choice with no land or coin to support him. At that time the whispers of the Jomsvikings were strong and though they numbered many they were yet to be unified under one King. The stirrings over the land were saying that the Danish King had plans and this bothered Holger. Why Jarl Brynjar had started to forego his duties as Jarl of the region was dumbfounding. Holger suspected that Brynjar not only lusted after the legend of the ring but failing he ever found it and harnessed it he would ally himself with a more powerful force than Greycloak. The petty Kingdoms were constantly at war with one another it had been so since Holger could remember.

"He is dead?"

"Ja, a long time dead. You should know many things about these men Thorik."

Grani snorted prompting Thorik on. "What?"

Holger looked at the boy and decided that the truth was all that would suffice. He was foolish to think that a strong spirit was all he required. The boys ragged appearance raised a new protective feeling in him that no doubt came from thoughts of his own son. Settling in a cross legged posture Holger released the sword strapped to his back and rested it over his legs.

"Well." He began. "First you must be of age and then you must face the Holmgang. You know what this is?" The boy shook his head. "It is a fight, a battle between two men, he who wishes to enter and a man already a Jomsviking. Nothing will do but death for either party unless the leader halts the fight if both men are worthy."

The Jarl's guard smiled, Thorik saw that thought the teeth were bright a few were chipped on one side and he wondered if a fist had caught him, then continued.

"There is a code all Jomsviking live by, tis strict and violation comes with a price, break the code and punishment is expulsion… depending on the crime." Holger smiled again at the frightened look in the boy's eye. "Honour and oaths are all important. You are bound to your brother and sworn to protect them and defend them in battle. You will never speak ill of your fellow man or quarrel however… they are men after all and as such cannot be expected to turn away if provoked.

So young Thorik say a man, a Jomsviking brother, casts ill words on your character or accuses you of a crime what then? Even the fastest of men will feud over something at one time. Should you feud with another your commander will decide whether you fight out a resolution for it is forbidden to raise your own hand in blood fury."

Thorik considered this for a moment and thought of the two men Ari and Dag. Had they sworn such allegiance to each other, how was it they travelled alone, and what was their mission. He wished he knew all of these things and much more.

"So Thorik think you want still to be a Jomsviking?"

"Ja!" Thorik spluttered awakening from his own thoughts. He glanced at Grani whose eyes were now fixed on the man.

"Hah! Well more you should hear. Now you are a warrior?" Holger wagged a finger at the boy and winked. He was enjoying talking to Thorik much in the way he would his own son. "A Jomsviking may never show fear in the face of his enemy, whether he be of equal strength or weaker, but should he be outnumbered and only then is it acceptable to retreat and live to fight another day.

You might become a rich man if you live long enough Thorik for the spoils of war are shared between all men. Gold, horses, land, but would you enjoy them knowing where your wealth came from?" A shadowy memory crept into the forefront of Holger's memory, his brother gravely changed from his travels, it was a sad thought.

"Know this lastly…" Holger's voice became grave and pained. "No wife may you ever take as your own, no woman or child may you protect within the safety of the keep, so long as you are Jomsviking. Should you wish to travel alone only a few days you will be given and no more, so best you use it to make your farewells from the life you knew."

The boy shuddered, it was a sad ending to the tale, and he felt the heavy weight of something more than the man spoke of filling the space between them. "Is it forever?" He asked.

"Is what forever?" Holger shot a look at Thorik puzzled by his question.

"When you give them your word? You can never leave?"

"Ah." Again another memory surfaced forcing Holger to stifle a grimace threatening to wash over his face. "Tis not known to any other than the Jomsvikings. Though let me tell you this… such men do not often live long enough Thorik to regret their chosen path. These men are hired to fight and as such life is forfeit… nothing is forever."

"I think mayhap I prefer to have the choice." Thorik spoke holding the gaze of the grey stallion locked in its black pools of obsidian.

"Choice…" Holger grumbled. Rubbing his hand across his chin he considered it.

The boy made a real and unsettling point. There was a choice to be made and Holger was fast approaching the impasse of his own life. His wife and children were living deep in the confines of Srovberget and their movements would be noticed at once as Jarl Brynjar trusted no-one. Even being his closest guard Holger knew the deep jealousy Brynjar had over him, since Holger a lesser man of impoverished birth had sired children while Brynjar's women lay barren. It irked Holger that the Jarl was unlike many men he had met that valued the work and sweat it had taken to have come as far as he had. There were many who valued their progression and the taking of a wife and creation of a line were all that truly mattered. It made him wonder if children would only become another possession of the man devoid of love.

But what use did Brynjar have for love? Holger felt himself grow desperately unhappy with his situation. He knew what he wanted to do but not how to achieve it without causing possible harm to his family. Then there was Solvieg to consider, he had sworn to her to help in any way he could. Short of helping her and Inge conspire he had done little to keep her from the harsh uncompromising ways of her husband. Solvieg was a kind soul who had been dealt a weak hand. She was the sole child of deceased parents and her own surviving kin lived far from Srovberget. Holger watched her often and wondered how alone and miserable she really felt. Many women married to the like of a man such as Brynjar at least had the comfort of children to raise.

Holger set his mind to the facts. He had sent a man to the Jarl apprising him of the situation. He had two men with him, who though proved little better than tavern hounds were still men with iron and capable of putting up a fight if need be. He had caught the boy and the horses. The advantage was his except for the location of the men. He had to change the course of the game to his advantage once more, but first he had a decision to make, what would his next move be?

"Thorik… what does your heart tell you to do?" Holger asked the boy with a blank expression.

Thorik swallowed and could not tell what the right answer was to give the man. At length he spoke giving him all he could trust himself to be true. "It tells me the men need their horses. It tells me they are more than Jomsvikings." Then sharing a look with the horse he said. "It tells me to be honourable to myself."

The guard looked at the boy astounded. He had often heard that children could say what men feared to. That they possessed the innocence to know what was right and wrong and question all. But his own children had never been placed in a position to answer such a question and so the boy's honesty shook him.

"Come with me!" Holger stood and grabbed a line of rope lying in the sand. Without a word he pulled Thorik to his feet and quickly bound his wrists. Then he shouted to his men before fastening his cloak about his shoulders and the leather strap of his sword belt. The two men raced to the scene with relieved faces that there was nothing amiss.

"Change of plan." Holger strode over to Grani and released his reins from the post wedged in the dirt. "The boy has spoken, I have the location of the men, I will continue ahead while you return to Srovberget by way of Gulafjord and make contact with the Jarl."

"Gulafjord? That lies in the opposite direction of Srovberget. It will add days travel… should we not…" One man spoke.

"Nei! We must ensure there are no others seeking to join them, keep your eyes open, suspect any who look out of place." Holger barked. "Once Brynjar receives word we have located the men he will understand my thinking, he has come close to capturing the woman before, a few days will make no difference we must be careful. Should you discover more of their kind then you split and one remains in the fjord at the Thing and the other to the Jarl. Tell him I will return with the woman or the heads of the men. Either way I will return."

"He won't like this Holger I am sure of it, and you are one man! We've seen such men as these." The young man spoke.

"My strength and fighting are in question Agar?" Holger raised a heavy eyebrow before lifting Thorik onto Grani's back.

"Nei… nei." The man raised his hands.

"At least take one of us. And why take the boy?" The other man offered.

"Bait… and he knows the way." With a swift jump Holger sat upon Grani's back. "Do as I say!"

The men nodded and took the reins of the remaining horses. Walking them over to their own steeds the men each took a torch and turned to make their way back to Gulafjord.

Thorik gulped as Holger reached forward and handed him a small blade. "Cut your bonds, I trust you will tell me where they are for I mean to aid them, do not think to lie to me Thorik. I am a man of my word and my family's lives depend on your honesty and mine. Now where are they?"

Rubbing his raw delicate wrists Thorik saw the flash of a blade but felt his heart still as he recognised it as his own. The man had given him back his sword.

"They are in Giffni."

Holger brought Grani to a slow walk and they made their way along the beach in the moonlight. "Where is Giffni?" He asked.

"Tis along the coast, only fishermen and the settlements near there use that name anymore, there are many caves and cliffs it can be treacherous or a safe harbour."

"Then lead the way Thorik."

"Do you really think more Jomsviking are following them?"

"Nei, I said that to buy us time."

The boy twisted to look at the man sitting astride Grani behind him. His gaze was fixed ahead and gingerly Thorik raised a finger to point and the horse broke into a gallop.

# 9.

Liv strained to hear the muffled voices, her eyes opened to a dimly lit cavern, around a fire three shapes sat. Lifting her head wearily she groaned as her stiff muscles cried out in agony. Succumbing to the need for rest she slumped back down on the fur bedding beneath her. One of the figures stood by the fire while another quickly appeared by her side soothing her brow with a damp rag and muttering soft words.

"Rest... you must rest." Gytha whispered.

Feeling nothing but confusion Liv struggled and rolled onto her side, propping her body up with an elbow. "Who are you? Where..."

"Liv, sleep, you are in Giffni." Ari's voice came from behind the woman and Liv saw the man Dag hovering in the background.

Gytha ushered the men back to the fire with her hand turning back to her ward. "You have been ill, the blow to your head was worse than it seemed but you are mending, we travelled here by boat. I am Gytha, Dag brought me to heal you, wait I'll fetch some water."

Liv watched the young woman return to the men nodding at Ari, who had a worried look on his face. Seeing the young woman relate something to him, his eyes rested upon Liv allowing a faint smile to cross over his mouth. Dag darted his stare between the two eventually nodding to Liv and slapping Ari on the shoulder. At length the two men returned to their conversation with Ari glancing over his shoulder as Gytha returned to Liv's side.

"He has feared for you. He has been by your side, sometimes he spoke as I told him it helps the soothe those in a deep sleep." Gytha smiled. "Do you remember aught?"

"I wish I did." Liv smiled sadly. She wished to know what Ari had said while she was unconscious. "How long have we been here?"

"In Giffni two nights, you much improved with the heat of the caves, truly it is a remarkable place."

"Ja… a sanctuary… the caves are a warren we will be safe here awhile."

"As Ari said." Gytha lifted the skin to Liv's lips and nodded with a set stare as Liv thanked her. "You are a guardian?"

Sucking in a breath Liv narrowed her eyes and furrowing her brow pushed the skin back to the woman. "I know not what you speak of…"

"You are branded."

"Many former slaves are."

"Not with Yggrasil!" Gytha whispered harshly. "Your name too it means protector of life."

"We all bear the namesakes of the Gods."

"The markings on your body." Gytha scrutinized Liv as she saw the woman realise for the first time her garments had been removed and she lay in a tunic covered with blankets.

"Who removed my clothing?"

"I did… you were in dire need of a bath… I saw the markings who made them?"

"I don't know you…"

"You can trust me Liv, I'm a healer, I came with these men to ensure you survived. You've been through much and your body was near to giving up. Please allow yourself to trust me."

The young woman smiled warmly at Liv who felt too tired to argue. "Tis a long story."

"We have time, the horses won't be here for a few days, time for all to talk I think." Gytha cast a look over her shoulder to the men. She had not had much of a chance to speak with Dag but when the moments had arisen, he was his usual humour laden self even managing to raise a laugh now and again from Ari. "And… I had a vision of you when we were at the farmstead… who is the boy?"

Closing her eyes Liv felt a pang of hurt stab at her heart. "That I cannot tell you Gytha."

"Then say what you can." Gytha folded her legs beneath her and edged a little closer to Liv. The cave was warm and her patient appeared comfortable on the makeshift bed of furs.

"Many a year now I've had to run. The markings, were made by the Volur women under the instruction of the Yggdrasil Kynslod, they are spells. The branding a mark from the Kynslod given to me by my own guardian but he is gone now." Liv paused. "Has Ari seen?"

"Yes, he helped me remove your clothing."

"Ah…" Liv turned her head away and felt ashamed. He must have wondered who administered the tattoos and she knew he had an understanding of the runes. Her fingers trailed the line of small fine markings etched into her skin on her right arm. There were bands of runes on her wrists and down her right leg and on her back a script ran down her spine. The night the marks had been made she suffered much pain, the ink was tainted with viper venom and she had slipped into a delirium that caused terrible visions. Her guardian had helped to hold her down as she wept, the Volur tapping the needle over and over into her flesh, the women whispered their incantations evoking the will of the Gods.

"He was not repelled. There is not much that would keep him from you." Gytha ventured, realising with a wide smile that this was just what the woman needed to hear.

"Markings are one thing…" She sighed. "His ire towards me is gone?"

"Ja, was more hurt than anger. His life continued too while you were parted… you should talk… mayhap the chance will arrive in the morn?"

Liv sighed and stretched her body beneath the blankets. "Gytha thank you for your work you are gifted. You mentioned visions… are you Volur?"

"Nei."

"What did your vision tell you?"

"I'll speak of it when you are ready to speak of the boy. Liv, Ari thinks him dead why do you not set that to right?"

"Trust Gytha… I did not know he was Ari when we met. There wasn't an opportunity to tell him anything. I think perhaps you all know one another better than I do right now."

"Not Ari!" Gytha chuckled knowingly. "In the morn I will gather herbs and roots my supplies need tending… mayhap Dag will help… he looks the foraging sort!"

Liv looked at the woman and burst into laughter that filled the cave. The two men looked up from the fire, then to one another not understanding the joke. Gytha was a fair face to look upon Liv thought and she could see why Dag would have taken an interest. It was not such a great leap to assume the woman felt the same. The maid had long thick flaxen hair, large round eyes of the deepest blue and a short sharp nose.

Suddenly the pounding in Liv's head returned and nausea rolled in her stomach. Groaning, she raised a hand to her damp brow.

"Where are you from?" Gytha asked, looking over Liv's features.

"My mother was a thrall who died from my birth. My father came from a nomad tribe but I do not know him             ." Struggling to speak the words Liv's voice trembled, licking her lips, she closed her eyes.

"You sought him out?" Gytha saw the waxen expression on the woman's face and guessed she was not completely out of the woods. She probed her to keep talking while she dropped a few herbs from her pouch into a small cup. From the water skin, she mixed the contents and lifted the vessel to Liv's lips watching her drink without question.

"Nei…" It was a lie, but Liv would not reveal too much of herself to the perceptive woman no matter how well at ease she was starting to become in her company. She knew her features often raised an eyebrow, she was fair of skin but dark of hair, her eyes were almond shaped and a curious mixture of colours they were neither blue nor green or brown. She was unlike the northern women, but shared many of their qualities. Strong and brave and if pushed to fight would give her best, especially with what she had to protect. Given the chance she might have made a good wife with a prosperous home and born strong sons but that would never be now.

"Your mother you say she was thrall?"

"Ja but not by Ari's Chieftain. She still wore her collar when she died, but spoke a few words that were later told to me. She had a foreign tongue… she spoke of my father but never gave a name only a place." Liv snapped her mouth shut and gritted her teeth. She felt stupid and cursed herself thinking only that the weariness in her body and mind had caused her to say too much. A slow burning had begun in her stomach, its quelling ceased, the ache in her head began to die a little. Her eyes began to droop and her breathing slowed to a steady peaceful slumber.

Gytha raised a hand and stroked the woman's shoulder. "My parents died some time ago and I was left in the care of my brother, a stupid, foolish man, I hope never to return and in truth I cannot for he would see fit to beat me. Until you three I was close to despair, our lives take strange paths sometimes."

With that Gytha stood and rejoined the men momentarily before taking her place on her own set of furs a few feet from where Liv lay. Liv dragged her eyes open watching as Dag let his gaze linger a while on the healer before turning back to Ari.

Considering Gytha's words Liv closed her eyes and let her ears drink in the soft noises of the cavern, the men spoke at length, but she could not hear definition in the sounds and gave up straining her ears. It had been a trying time and against her better judgement she let the safety provided by the group rest her soul for a few hours at least.

The darkness that had come over her in her unconscious state had seemed like mere seconds fractured only by vague memories of being on horseback and rocking motion of being aboard a small vessel. Gingerly Liv stroked her jaw and ear, she wanted to know how bruised and cut her face was but did not know if the healer would carry a polished metal disk so often used to observe ones features.

Hours later, though feeling like mere moments Liv awoke to see the room slightly dimmed from the light provided by the fire and small oil lamps, the men appeared to have sought the comfort and rest of their own furs, for a moment Liv imagined herself alone. The muscles in her chest loosened a little and she pushed herself onto her elbows, looking around the floor space she saw three separate forms apparently sleeping, silently Liv stood with a slight wobble. A feeling of lightheadedness lingered before she tentatively took a few steps. Her hair fell forward as she bent slightly, resting her hands on her knees before taking a deep breath and stepping closer to the waning fire. The thin tunic she wore and her skin smelled of lavender and something that reminded her of a spice called frankincense she had once encountered in a market. It felt good to be clean and free from her ragged clothes, though she wondered where they might be.

Stooping to the fire she sat and pulled her knees up to her chest. Stretching her hands, she rotated her wrists and flexed her fingers above the heat of the embers. Not far from her position she spied her clothes drying on a large rock and a smile crossed her lips as she thought of a distant memory from a time when she and Ari had come to Giffni in the past.

"Liv?" Ari approached and stood a moment, waiting for the woman to acknowledge him. Blinking wearily he saw her smile and took a seat. "Gytha says you are healing?"

"Ja… though I do not feel myself." Rubbing her temples, she feared the throbbing would make an unwanted return. "Thank you Ari."

"For what?" Ari glanced at her with a puzzled expression.

"Bringing me here, for Gytha's help, you didn't have to."

"Nei…" He sighed dragging a hand across his forehead. "I had to."

Liv looked at Ari and felt a terrible pang of sadness strike her heart. He seemed so unlike the man she had once known, she fought the urge to hold him and instead sat feeling the pull to him stretch to snapping, his eyes were full of a history she knew nothing about.

"Ari I don't know what to say or do."

"Nor I."

They sat in silence, looking at one another. Ari observed the woman and started to recognise the traits he had once known. She was quiet and oblivious to her beauty even now covered in scratches and bruises. Liv sat chewing on her lip which he knew was in frustration and nervousness. As a younger woman she had done this when deep in thought or when she worried over something. Her brow slightly creased and he guessed she was wrestling with the same questions he had. He felt terribly guilty about his behaviour when finding her but what could he have done? He had sought to know who she had become without her knowing it was he who had found her. Ari had needed to see the raw honesty of her life now, not clouded by what they had once shared together. He had believed her heartless and selfish, he had blamed her for the choices he had made because of a broken heart and wounded pride, but now he knew differently and wondered why she had been lied to. It occurred to him that she was still being lied to but he could not reveal that mistruth until she was stronger.

"I would have come for you always." He whispered sadly staring at his hands on his lap. They were hands that had done terrible things in the past six years, hands that had learned how to fight better and kill quicker, hands that had earned him the name of Gorm Swift-Axe and helped him to vent his fury. How could she understand?

"You must know I thought you dead, I don't know why he lied to me, but Ari it was worse than that…"

"How?" His eyes shot upwards to meet her opal gaze.

"The reason I can't return with you to our home."

"There is none?"

"Ja there is… Harvardr told me you died in the fire they all believed I started, I saw the flames I heard the screaming, I swear it wasn't me."

Ari glared, a rage swelled in his chest, but subsided as quickly as it came, and she looked at him fear written over her delicate features. "No Liv, do not think my anger is for you." Crouching he laid a hand on her shoulder and felt an old feeling tingle in his fingertips. "Do you speak of the fire in the woman's workhouse?"

"Ja." She looked away.

"Nei Liv, such lies you have been told and I don't know why. I am here before you now, how could you think any would blame you for my death?"

"I heard the screaming, Harvardr said he heard the women say it was me that started the blaze and it had killed you in the process. They said I was evil and unworthy, that I had witnessed you with another and taken terrible vengeance."

Shocked Ari removed his hand and rubbed his jaw with the back of his hand. New whiskers had sprouted since last he shaved causing him to scratch his chin in thought. This was all new and strange information, he could not understand Harvardr's motives. The old man had always been a friend to his people, he could only surmise that he had needed Liv and guessed she would not be easily moved without coercion. The markings on her body and the branding were signs of seidr magic, something Liv had never shown and interest in that he knew of.

"There is much to talk about, but you must know that although you heard screaming there was not one life lost in the fire, trust me we were all confused when we discovered you gone. It was thought you had been lost in the fire until we discovered no bodies and I found the necklace on your pallet. It was then I realised you had run…"

"But not from you Ari."

"No."

"I am sorry you thought it so." Liv stared hard at his face before tearing her eyes away and closing them to stop the stinging. There was a part of her that felt anger he could so easily believe she would run, but what else could he have thought? What lies had been offered to him she wondered. Looking back at him she began to recognise the man before her. The same pale eyes of the coldest winter sky, his strong, straight nose and square jaw. His hair was still the colour of the fine leather saddles of their Chieftain's horses and his skin bore the same hue from many days in the sun. She saw faint lines around his eyes and mouth and felt warm to know that he did at least smile now and again though she had yet to see it herself. But there was a face behind the one before her where sadness and darkness lingered and she knew she too wore the same expression from time to time.

"I would see you smile?" She asked and lifted a hand to cup his face.

Taking her hand Ari kissed the palm, letting a small smile tug at his mouth. "And I you."

Liv knelt forward and kissed Ari before wrapping her arms around him in a tight embrace. Initially Ari's back stiffened in surprise, but feeling the familiar embrace of the woman he had loved terribly his resolve melted and hungrily he held onto her form.

For some minutes they sat entwined in one another's arms. Regretfully Ari broke away lifting Liv's chin with a finger, returning her soft kiss he rested his forehead against hers and breathed in the sweet floral scent of Gytha's soap on her skin. He was eternally grateful to the healer as more than once it occurred to him that Liv could have succumbed to her injuries, he might well have lost her once more after only finding her, which would have been too great a pain to bear.

"How long do we have here?" She whispered.

"A day or two more, mayhap a third, long enough to hear both our tales."

"So much to say… there are things you must know Ari… more you must know."

"Ja… there is much I must tell you but first we have this moment just to sit by the fire the way we once did." Ari pulled an arm around Liv's shoulders and drew her into his chest. Leaning back against the rolled blankets he used as a rest he and Liv lay for some time. They spoke of Giffni and the time they had once spent there each feeling the pull of one another and letting it pass. Each feeling it was too soon and hesitant to try a return to what they once had, slowly a dreamless sleep washed over them both.

# 10.

Dag listened to the voices until they became softer and then all together quiet. He was on watch and allowed Ari to rest with Liv in his arms for many hours. His friend was in need of proper sleep and it appeared his soul was at peace for now. As the time silently passed he kept his mind alert by practicing moves he would later use when next he and Ari played Tafl.

Of late the men had had little opportunity to play for any length of time and it was a game that required patience and tact. Dag carried the latticed board Ari had made for him in thanks. Over time he had exchanged the wooden pieces for soapstone and carved intricate details on each marker. The board was a treasured gift that replaced the one Dag's father had given him as a young boy. That board had been destroyed by another man whom Dag had crossed paths with and lost a fist fight to. It had surprised him that Ari would do such a thing since the gesture was greater than he required. He would have accepted the friendship in kind and in the years that followed they had formed a strong kinship to one another.

To join the Jomsvikings was no easy task, entry required a battle with an established soldier. Young men often died trying to become one, and the older men who perhaps fled their previous lives or were seeking to hide faired no better. The first months were tougher yet, training was all that filled their days, small groups formed within the ranks, but trust was an earned privilege that Dag found hard to find. He met Ari when the young man was sprawled on the ground after being set upon by a group of men, one of the group Hasti was no more than a drunkard and a lout. Hasti had accused Ari of theft and dishonour, Dag knew the man to be a liar and that most likely whatever he had said was taken from him had been lost in an ill advised dice game sodden with ale and wine. It was against the code to attack one of your own but like everything in life it was subject to interpretation.

Dag had weighed into the fray and pulled the battered Ari to his feet. The pair threw blows to the other men, slamming their fists into faces and ribs, using their feet to kick knees from their joints and winding the guts of the men. They walked away with pride and the blood of the attackers on their knuckles. The rest of the men nodded in approval, the older Jomsvikings would accept no less a reaction to an attempt on their names. Men had to fight and these new recruits had proved a measure of their worth.

Each player had a number of pieces on the Tafl board, one player however had fewer but possessed the king who started in the centre of the board. The objective of the king was to escape to a corner of the board while the opposite player tried to capture him. Some men used dice to increase the risk and potential of winning coin, other men usually the older men used their wits and threw riddles at one another. That was how Dag's father and uncle had played when he was a boy. To Dag it was a method he would show Ari when they were old with wives and children. There would then be time to enjoy the game better or so Dag thought. He realised very quickly that the life of a Jomsviking was short and swift but he had saved enough coin to pay his way out of the ranks and purchase land.

Dag was not sure where this dwelling of the future might be but he had come to appreciate Ari's tales of his homeland and he had not come across any other place that suited him more.

Gytha stirred on her furs and stretched, opening her eyes she looked around the cave and then to Dag, smiling she raised a finger to her lips and pointed to the two figures together by the fire. Nodding his head Dag signalled for her to sleep for another hour or two. Gytha smiled in response letting her eyes take in the dark hair and gaze of the warrior she had grown to trust. Turning on her side, she breathed in the earthy scent of the fur feeling at ease.

Returning to the game play in his mind Dag absently let his eyes drift over the sleeping body of the woman. He knew he had let her under his skin but not quite as much as Liv had done with Ari. All the same it was a new experience, he was not entirely sure he enjoyed his appreciation of her for more than her form. He was used to having women appreciate him and reveled in it, but required nothing further and when he thought of a wife it was for the line he might create rather than love. But this young woman had shown him talents he did not possess himself and an understanding of the world, her world, that did not demonstrate treachery or scheming. True, she wanted to be free of her brother but she had hurt no-one in the process nor abused trust. This was quite different from the women he was used to dealing with for they all had something to gain, and this woman had had much to lose.

By the fire Dag heard Ari stir, the man rose and stretched before turning to see if his friend was awake, with a quick look the two men stood and made their way to the mouth of the cave. Silently they walked along a series of tunnels before reaching the air of the crisp morning.

"How you never became lost is a mystery." Dag cocked his head back the way they had come.

"It took some time, but Liv marked the way with chalk, after a while we knew it without even a torch or lamp. Though I swear she can see in the dark like a cat."

"Her eyes say as much!" Dag grinned. "You spoke?"

"Ja and nei, we will speak today, I need to think it through before I start." Ari looked at his friend whose tanned complexion did not hide the rings of tiredness beneath his eyes. "Go sleep I will take watch."

Dag nodded. "Ja an hour or two is all I need. I will take Gytha to the wood for herbs and roots, then perhaps to explore the caves or a swim in the hot springs?"

Ari chuckled to himself and from under his breath muttered a curse before slapping Dag on his shoulder. "You know well your herbs and roots?"

"Ha! A clever man knows a little about a lot!" Flashing his wide grin he turned and headed back to his furs. He knew Ari would stand watch outside for as long as Dag needed to rest, but in truth he was eager to embark on his day with Gytha. Forcing himself to rest, he slowed his breathing and willed each muscle to ease.

When at last he awoke it was to a wide eyed Gytha shaking his shoulder roughly. Swatting her hand away, he wiped the sleep from his eyes and looked about the room. Laying a hand to his side, he felt his axe.

"What?!" He grunted.

"Gods above Dag! Tis Liv, she will not awaken!"

Dag came to his senses all at once staring with confusion at the healer. "What?"

"I can not rouse her, her skin is almost cold to the touch, where is Ari?" The woman spoke quickly.

"Wait I will fetch him." Dag stood and disappeared into the tunnel.

Gytha quickly scrambled back to the fire where Liv lay slumped against one of the men's packs. Her face wore the mask of the dead, but her breathing betrayed signs of life yet. Dark circles had formed beneath her eyes, her skin grey, the pulse in her neck slow and shallow.

The men returned to the chamber. Under Gytha's instruction Ari Lifted Liv back to her furs before turning to the young woman.

"What has happened? We spoke last night she seemed well." His eyes bore no accusations, but were full of questions.

Swallowing against a dryness forming in her throat Gytha grasped her leather bag and emptied its contents searching furiously through the pile of herbs roots and small lined bouquets of medicine.

"I think..mayhap…" Still scrabbling through her belonging she felt Ari grasp her wrist, jerking her gaze to his. "The daudr sovn!"

"Nei!" Ari dropped Gytha's hand swinging his gaze from Liv to Dag. He had heard tell of the daudr sovn among his men, but never witnessed it for himself. Many a man had fallen by his sword and axe, many a man he had seen slain in battle, these men died where they lay breathing their last before his eyes.

"Ive tried to waken her but she barely breathes. The pupils of her eyes are almost grey." Gytha's voice trembled.

"The dead sleep?" Dag breathed. "But how?"

"Injuries we cannot see?" Gytha's voice trembled. "Ari I cannot heal her here, I don't have what I need, how far are we from your home?"

"Too far." His voice was cold and flat.

"There is a healer there? Mayhap they have what Gytha needs?"

Dag offered.

"Too far." Ari dropped to his knees beside Liv. She did truly look like she was dying. He knew who could possibly help but he had no trust for this person now and knew Liv may resent him terribly for not having told her sooner. A firm hand grasped his shoulder, pulling his gaze away. Dag glared down at him.

"Odin's eye man! Wake up! What choice is there? Are we hours or days away?"

Shaking his head Ari stood and faced his friend. "A day but that's after we get across the causeway, it's at least half a day from here. There may be one who can do something, but I cannot be certain…"

"Is there time?" Dag questioned Gytha still kneeling at his feet surrounded by her supplies.

"It is the daudr sovn it can take her at any time or… she might lay like this for days or more. She is weak Dag."

Sagging his shoulders Dag turned away and brusquely tugged and his hair. Ari sighed heavily throwing his axe to the ground, the rock that bore Liv's clothing and her belongings sat undisturbed though tattered and torn he wished terribly she would rise from the bed and don her clothing ready for the new day. Gytha trembled, her hands shaking, she began to gather her supplies tossing them back into her leather bag, her fingers strayed over the items searching for something to help.

A small root poked from beneath a small bundle of linen squares. She had not remembered gathering it but recognised it all the same. Gasping she lifted it carefully bringing it to her eyeline.

"Ari…" She whispered. "Belladonna!"

"Madness!" Dag barked. "It will kill her!"

"Nei Dag, it will keep her heart beating long enough for us to reach Smols. The root is the most potent part of it, I can brew an elixir." Now looking at Ari she stood. "It is not without risk, I cannot promise…"

"Do it!" Lifting his axe from the ground, he tucked it into the loose leather belt about his blue tunic and turned to face Dag. "Let's gather our things."

Nodding Dag swiftly moved to roll up and tie the bedding furs. Ari filled the small kettle on the smouldering fire with water from a skin for Gytha who had set about grinding her root in a small soapstone pestle from her sack.

Silently the men cleared the chamber of their belongings to the mouth of the tunnel. As Ari threw down his pack Dag grabbed his forearm.

"By the God's Ari…"

"I know." Ari nodded and slapped his friend's shoulder, but before he could rejoin Gytha and ask about her progress a sound from the tunnels strayed to his ear. Dag too stiffened and scented something on the cool breeze filtering from the morning air outside.

Ari reached the cave mouth, exiting the tunnels he saw a mist had fallen over Giffni. A light fog gathered at their feet and the damp smell of rain hung heavy in the air. He had expected their visitors to have concealed themselves in the wood watching and waiting when no attack had presented itself in the warren of the tunnels. The scent that had floated on the air betrayed that of the horses, but age and experience told Ari to be wary in thinking the boy had arrived so swiftly. The sight that greeted him pleased him initially, hope sprung in his chest until he realised that though Thorik had indeed arrived he was not alone.

Dag appeared behind Ari almost walking into him as he had stopped abruptly. When he saw what his friend was looking at anger flared causing him to bare his teeth at the man standing beside the fisherman's boy.

"The Jarls man?" Dag growled moving round the solid pillar of Ari to stand at his side. This was not what they needed now his mind raged.

"Ja… Holger is it?" Ari barked at the man.

Thorik stood darting a scared expression between the man and the two Jomsvikings. Like predatory animals they started to separate and move around them in opposite directions. Each gripped an axe in their sword arms, their frames poised to attack, still dressed in their dark blue tunics leather trousers and boots they looked fearsome even without their chainmail and armour. Feeling scared Thorik shrank back from the men he had so admired sensing they might set upon Holger without realising he had helped him.

"Stop!" The boy cried out.

Dag looked at the boy, but Ari stayed focused on Holger. The Jarls man lowered his own sword to the ground slowly and stood, raising his hands in front of him.

"He is the Jarls man!" Dag shouted. "How many have you brought with you?" He directed his question to the man.

"None!" Thorik shouted back before Holger could open his mouth.

Dag fired a wrathful glance at the boy and strode towards him. Shaking Thorik by the scruff of his shirt he glared at the boy. Wide eyed Thorik feared the trembling threatening to shake his limbs from his body.

"Leave him be!" Holger growled. Eyeing the two men he saw their training, their fierceness, but also something else. He and the boy had happened upon them without a chance to alert them of his own presence, surprising them, however their furrowed brows looked etched with worry.

Hearing the man Dag narrowed his eyes and shot a look at Ari, who now stood mere feet from Holger.

"Explain!" Ari growled keeping his eyes locked on the man.

"He is the Jarls man no longer! He wants to help, he brought me here with Grani, he sent the other men back to the Jarl." Thorik raced through his words. Stopping for a breath, he saw the Dag kick Holger's sword away standing squarely before them with his arms folded across his chest. Ari had rested the axe in the crook of his folded arms and stood looking intently at Holger.

"We have met." Ari spoke.

"Ja, briefly, when my Jarl hired your captain. You were given the task to find the woman and the boy."

Ari nodded, but Dag grunted. "So he speaks? I thought Thorik spoke for you!" Firing a dirty look at the young boy Dag saw the heat of shame flush in his cheeks and ground his teeth in annoyance.

"How came you by our Thorik?"

"Wasn't easy, the boy near outran us, we found him on the beach." Holger replied.

"It was only when I let the horses rest!" Thorik cried, feeling suddenly like he must defend himself.

"Why should we believe what he says?" Ari jerked his chin in the direction of the boy. "You now decide to leave your Jarls side? Why?"

"Many reasons… but for the one that concerns you I can no longer follow a madman who seeks out legends and hunts down women and children."

"Honourable." Dag hissed, his voice laden with sarcasm.

"Tis the truth. I have a wife and children, they deserve better than Jarl Brynjar. I made haste with the boy here and ask of your services."

"Hah!" Dag grinned at Ari. "He wants us to work for him!" Shaking his head, he fired an angry look to Holger. "You don't have the coin!"

Holger shrugged, lowering his hands, he stood looking at Thorik. "My family are all to me and if you kill me they will suffer in Srovberget. Release me and I will employ others of your kind to free them from the Jarls grip, if I fail in that they again will suffer. There is only one chance for a life with them. I must find a way to bring them to me. There can never be a life for us when I work for the Jarl and when he discovers my treachery he will be wrathful." Holger's throat grew tight at his own words. He had hoped the men would listen, but something told him that they were ready to bind the rope around his wrists and throw him over the side of the cliff.

"And if we do decide to kill you?" Ari spoke at last reading the man's thoughts. "It appears you have risked much to come here. But why not return with your men to the Jarl instead of aiding the boy? What proof is there of your change of heart?"

Holger drew a breath and studied the face of the warrior in front of him. He seemed less angry and dark than when they first met. He had made an impression on Holger then, he was proud and strong, this man still young but his vocation had taught him much. He was right of course, Ari, what proof did Holger have other than his word?

"The boy brought me to my senses." Holger said. "I had to help him… to find you and warn you of the Jarl's intentions."

"What?" Thorik gasped. Pride washed over him for a moment before the dark looks of the men continued against one another.

"Intentions of the Jarl?" Ari spoke through gritted teeth. "His intentions were clear when he employed us."

"Nei… he is more determined than ever, you think he will not follow you? That he does not have his ways to find you? No man can disappear entirely… no woman either." Holger rasped and pulled a heavy hand through his long beard. "Look at the lad. He is a waif, but his heart is strong, he reminded me that we are more than what we appear to be." Holger held Ari's gaze. It was unyielding and betrayed no emotion. The other man Dag looked interested now instead of angry, but this did not necessarily mean anything positive for Holger. "Kill me or do not. Free me or do not. All I care about is my family, I will find a way to help them whether it be breathing in this life or the next."

"You seem eager to die?" Dag said dryly.

"You give up so easily?" Ari asked, nodding in agreement with his friend.

"I am tired. The bitterness and hatred, the lusting after legends of wealth, the warring of the Kingdoms. Brynjar will bring disaster to us all, even now he flaunts his disregard for our King by avoiding the Thing in Gulafjord, he lacks respect and I find none any longer for him."

"And you leave your family to this man in Srovberget?" Dag asked.

"I took my chance to act now." Holger eyed the man sadly before turning away to stare at the woods beyond.

Ari took a step back, gathering Thorik by the shoulders, he instructed him to take Grani by the reins and stand closer to the cave entrance, walking to Dag he questioned him with his eyes. Dag shrugged, grinding his teeth he looked at the Jarls man, clearing his throat he lowered his tone.

"I cannot say, you?"

"Nei. But either we take him or kill him. He believes the Jarls men will follow, even if we can trust him who is to say their path is not already being tracked? I would not say he is a broken man, but there is regret. I believe he loves his family. Mayhap we buy his trust."

"Buy it?" Dag raised and eyebrow.

"Ja. We agree to help him, take him to the settlement, then decide what to do. We can't risk staying here any longer."

"And if Brynjar sends an army?" Dag sighed heavily.

"The village would never stand up to that kind of battle, they are farmers and fishermen, traders, the Chieftain rarely orders a raid unless need be. The men can wield an axe as good as any but soldiers they are not."

"Then mayhap we have a use for Holger after all? We must move, let us take him, we can talk on it later, we don't have the time right now." Dag threw a look at the boy who stood sheepishly stroking the muzzle of the fine grey horse.

"Nei... Liv." Ari kicked the earth and walked back to Holger with Dag. "Come."

Holger glanced warily at the men, but when they turned their backs to him and entered the mouth of the cave, the darker haired one guiding Thorik with him, he felt a little tension ease from his shoulders. The one he recognised as Gorm had lifted his sword from the earth taking it with him. It mattered not thought Holger, he still had his axe and Daggers. The men appeared to be neither intimidated nor overly concerned with him, making him pause. Had something happened, he wondered?

The darkness of the tunnel took him by surprise, stumbling over loose rocks on the cave floor Holger felt for the tunnel walls to steady his pace. Ahead he could hear the dark haired Jomsviking whispering to the boy while the other warrior strode ahead. Just as Holger's eyes were adjusting to the diminished light an amber glow began to seep into his vision and suddenly he found himself in a chamber. A small fire burned brightly and a smell of smoke gently scented the air. The room was warm and there was a feeling of moisture, Holger guessed there was a hot spring nearby.

The darker haired Jomsviking gruffly took Holger by the shoulder and led him to the fire, indicating he should sit then crouched beside him. "We need no trouble."

"None." Holger nodded.

"Thorik come sit here." Dag flicked a finger to the boy who stood at the chamber entrance chewing his lip and pulling at a stray thread on his cloak. "My name is Dag, he is Ari though you know him as Gorm." His words directed to Holger. "Thorik… watch him."

"Ja." Thorik frowned regretfully. But before Holger could raise a question Dag crossed the chamber where Ari stood talking to a young woman. The woman knelt on the ground and as she turned to meet the approach of Dag, Holger saw with surprise there was another woman laying on a bed of furs. Even with the warm orange glow of the embers filling the room Holger saw by her waxen appearance she was gravely ill.

"Her heart is strong but her breathing concerns me." Gytha worriedly darted a look at each man before staring at the new member of their group. "He's one of the Jarls men?"

"Ja." Ari nodded grimly. "If I take Grani and ride hard Liv will be within the village in a day."

"Do it." Dag grunted. "The man Holger will give me no problems be sure of that. We will continue on foot."

Feeling weariness threatening to rob him of his strength Ari roughly drew a hand across his whiskered jaw. "Damn it to Hel! Prepare her Gytha, Dag the way is not complicated, the causeway can be walked twice a day at sunrise and sunset. Make haste for the tide brings in the waters all too quickly. Once you reach the shoreline of Smols follow it until you reach pasture land, from there you will be in the shadow of Hornelen. Walk towards it until you reach the lake, it is large and will take you at least half a day to pass around it, I will return for you there where the forest meets the water's edge."

"If you are not there?"

"Blow your horn… I will hear it, but be careful the woods are home to wolves and I will not take the chance of losing you all to the hunger of a beast. Not now."

"If I didn't know you better I'd say that was good humour threatening." Dag suppressed a wry grin.

"Tis not the time my friend, but know this I'll be a sad man to find an old toothless wolf chewing on your leathery hide!" His thinly set grimace said nothing as Ari walked to their packs and disappeared to ready Grani for the task.

"Tis a good friendship." Gytha lifted her hand up to take Dag's from her seated position by Liv.

"Ja." Gently he smiled at her before walking back over to the fire where Holger and Thorik sat with pensive expressions.

# 11.

Grani moved swiftly for a horse that had already covered many a mile with two on his back. Now his long, graceful strong limbs set to work again riding out into the misty evening that covered Giffni. Ari guided the horse by memory along the path that stretched from the caverns on the cliff top to the rough shoreline leading to the causeway.

It took Ari all his might to hold Liv against his chest without her drooping, Dag had helped to lash a rope about her waist and his so she would stay atop Grani without coming to harm. The weight of her unconscious body caused him to draw breath 'how could she feel so heavy?' he wondered. The lapping of waves on the shingle as they cantered by caused Ari to nudge Grani into a gallop, the tide was coming in and the way to Smols would be lost till morning if he did not make haste.

Above him in the foggy sky a bird cawed. It was the first Ari had heard in some days since they had sought refuge in the caves. Giffni had always been a safe haven for them and now he fled with Liv back to Smols, back to the settlement, back to the one he now knew could not be trusted. But what choice did he have, Gytha for all her abilities was at a loss to heal Liv and Ari would be damned to an eternity in Hel before he lost her again. Part of him did not welcome this new feeling. He had spent so long hating her, wanting her to return, resenting what he thought was true. But he knew he had to let go of the past, it would serve him unjustly, he knew he must focus for there were new dangers. If this man Holger was to be trusted then Brynjar would find them, it would not be so hard Ari realised. He had his Jomsviking training to rely on but he and Dag were only two men.

He knew that the group behind him would move as swiftly as Dag could urge them to, on his own his friend had tireless energy running for days before he succumbed to weariness, Holger would be a fit man too though older than Dag. Gytha and the boy Thorik would slow them, but it could not be helped. Ari surmised they would be safe enough at present from the pursuit of the Jarl's men should they be advancing to Giffni. It was Holger he was unsure of, the man professed a hatred for Brynjar and a desire to flee with his family, his words had been reasonable but what judgment could Ari really make. In Brynjar's hall he had observed Holger from the corner of his eye. The man had stood behind his Jarl, stood in the shadows, watching and listening. Ari had felt Holger's eyes upon him, but no words had been exchanged until now.

Feeling the weight of Liv's pack on his back Ari shifted carefully in the saddle. Grani was picking his way across the causeway with care, should he slip or stumble it could mean a lame leg. The mists surrounding them hampered their progress and curses threatened to spill from Ari's mouth. When at last he could smell the pine from the trees on the shore of Smols he released a breath and kicked Grani into a quicker trot. Darkness was fast approaching and Ari knew that he would make little progress this evening. The best he could hope for was to reach the lake, there he would let Liv rest and administer more of Gytha's elixir. At first light he would make the journey around the lake, through the forest, and onto the settlement. By the next evening he would have her seen to and return for Dag and the others. He hoped he would reach them before Dag felt he needed to use his horn for although it would alert Ari to them it may also alert others.

The straps of the pack dug into Ari's shoulders pinching the skin beneath his woolen tunic and he grimaced at the tightness. It was a strong leather bag, but made for smaller shoulders than his. For the first time in many days he realised that somewhere concealed inside was the ring Liv was protecting and he felt the weight of it. He would not search though her things for it, it was not what he wanted, though he knew it would become part of a conversation they should have had by now. If only he had not been so full of ire towards her on the ship and missed the lackwit who sought to attack her. If only he had noticed the injury was more grievous than a smack to the head, what had he been thinking he groaned to himself.

This was part of the problem he realised, his years in the Jomsvikings had allowed him to fight and think only with a warriors mind naught else had been of interest to him. It had been stupidity on his part he knew now.

The mist parted for a moment like the heavy curtains that hung in his Chieftains longhouse, he saw a trail leading to the lake and pulled the reins to show Grani the way. They walked for some time before Ari recognised a ramshackle hut in a small clearing by the edge of the great lake of Smols. If the air had not been so filled with fog he would have seen Hornelen, his mountain.

It was said amongst his people that Odin the All-Father himself had stood atop it, striking his staff into the summit and causing the skies to fill with lightening. As he had done so the heavens of Gimli showered down their praise of his honour, turning the night sky into a wave of rainbows. Any warrior who had witnessed the rainbow sky at night knew he would meet an honourable end and be granted entry into Valhalla. Ari had seen such aura's in the blackness of the night, but had never felt certain about his future.

Untying the rope about their waists Ari gently slid from Grani's back and lifted Liv over his shoulder. Resting her on the soft grass of late summer he threw down the packs and guided Grani to water. Leaving the horse to drink his fill and eat the sweet green grass Ari inspected the hut. It was in a sorry state, clearly no-one had thought to maintain it in years. The wooden panels were blackened with mildew and rotten, the roof for the most part was intact, but one strong wind or whisper of a storm and he reckoned it would flatten instantly. Pushing against the timber of the small round structure he heard it ache and groan with pressure, but it stood fast enough for him to think it safe enough for a night.

The beaten earthen floor inside betrayed evidence of goats recently taking shelter. Looking outside Ari saw water rushes along the lake's edge, taking his Dagger he cut through a handful and used them as a makeshift broom to sweep away the rank droppings. Satisfied the hut was clean enough, he unrolled a blanket on the floor and laid Liv upon it. She stirred for a moment and tried to open her eyes, but swiftly returned to her unconscious state.

Gathering wood for a small fire did not take Ari long, striking his flint the first few sparks caught on the wood moss and smoke began to rise. From his pack he withdrew some dried meat and now stale flatbread chewing slowly. The water in his skin was lukewarm and so he drank from the freshwater stream flowing into the lake. Filling the skin with the sweet, cool water of Smols Ari allowed himself to feel at home for a moment. In some ways it was as if he had never left, but the reality was very different, he was a changed man now and had not seen his people in many years. He did not feel apprehension or fear of meeting with his family once more, his thoughts were clouded by the one he must ask to treat Liv.

Turning to face the hut where Liv lay he knew the shock of discovering the rude, foul tempered Jomsviking Gorm who had really been Ari had been too much, how would she react when she saw another familiar face? And in the weakened state she was now in. Regret and anger rose blood to his cheeks and Ari threw the skin down beside the hut, sinking down, he sat and looked out into the stillness of the night.

"Ari?" Liv whispered. Her voice was hoarse.

Spinning around Ari peered into the hut. "Liv? You are awake?"

"Where are we?"

"The lake of Smols."

"I feel weak, but my heart it rattles in my chest."

"Tis the daudr svon Liv, Gytha made a potion to keep it at bay but I must get you home, rest now for we have no choice but to wait for morning."

"The forest… wolves." Frowning slightly Liv stared at the shoddy wooden roof of the hut. She remembered Old Gunliek and his ragged herd of goats they would use for milk and cheese, she wondered if he still lived. Slowly her eyes fell upon Ari. "Come here."

Standing Ari stooped into the hut and drew to his haunches beside Liv. "Ja?"

"How came you by these scars?" Liv drew her eyes across fine trails of scars running from Ari's jaw down onto his neck. The amber flame from the fire illuminated the flecks in her opal eyes.

"Ah." Ari's eyes narrowed and his jaw ticked. He hated the scars almost as much as the telling of how they came to be. He thought it ugly for many a drunken tavern wench thought so, not that he cared aught what they thought truly. Scars were the way for a Viking man, what did he care if those women scolded him with cold unfeeling eyes, he would not marry them or see them again.

It was a fair question for Liv to ask, her own body was marred by the years they had spent apart. A branding and tattoo's, he knew the same women who had scolded his appearance would have had much to say about Liv's. Women were not meant to be guardian's or warrior's, they were not meant to fight or incur the wrath of men. Viking women were to raise the children, run the house in the absence of their man, prepare the food for feasting and long winters ahead. At least this was the thinking of their people in the settlement, but Ari had always known it would not have been a future such as this that he and Liv would share.

"It was a raven. It belonged to the fiercest warrior I have ever met... but do not let Dag know I said so. He would be aggrieved to think he is not the fiercest." Ari smiled and sat cross legged on the ground facing the doorway of the hut looking out onto Grani. "When I left our home I wandered for a time. Working on farmsteads, fishing, then I joined a ship... working for the captain of the ship that took us to Gulafjord. One night when we were docked a man came aboard looking for men who could fight and keep their mouths shut. I had nothing to lose and went with him. His name was Raki Gormsson."

Sighing Ari tossed a handful of dry leaves and bark onto the small fire, feeling Liv's eyes watching him he sighed and continued. "Raki was a strong man, as tall as he was broad, but he was ageing too. Had he lived, he would be older than my own father. When I met Raki he had wild white hair and a beard he braided, white as the winter snow it was, his skin was tanned and leathery like an old hide but his eyes I remember being brighter than a child's.

But the most remarkable thing about him was the raven that perched on his shoulder. It was called Muninn after Odin's bird. The bird had feathers blacker than coal, its eyes were pools of blackness, often I would dream about the bird's dark stare dreaming that I was drowning in their depths. Never had I seen such a man before nor since.

Two men left the ship with me to do Raki's bidding, it turned out that he had been searching for a man for a long long time. The man and Raki were bonded by a blood feud, it had raged on between their families for many a lifetime, the man had killed Raki's wife and children in hatred. Raki sought him out to kill him only, there was no other task greater than this, he paid us to trap the man so he would not lose him to escape again. Raki knew the man was hiding out on a nearby farm with his wife's people. No harm was to come to the family only the man.

We prepared ourselves one night in an empty barn next to the township's tavern. The other two men had gone to drink ale to slake their thirst after a long day's ride. When they returned, their faces were pale and they told Raki they would no longer work for him. They had discovered who the man was, they wished no part of the feud and refused coin for their troubles thus far. They tried to persuade me to leave but I would not hear of it."

"Muninn…" Liv murmured.

Lost in his thoughts Ari barely heard Liv but glanced at her face only to see her skin growing paler and the dark circles around her eyes increasing. He thought that it was perhaps a trick of the lack of light and the soft shadows thrown up from the glow of the fire. He decided to continue his tale if only to distract them both for a little longer. It occurred to Ari he had not thought of Raki for a very long time and he had sworn to himself never to let the memory of the man fade from his thoughts. He had taught Ari much.

"We made haste to the farm, but alas the man had disappeared. Raki raged and swore curses upon the Gods. He screamed at the women of the house, but they cried and threw their hands up in despair. They told him two men had approached and warned them of Raki's plans. We left them and rode out onto the hillside, from atop we could see the township's lights and ship's moored in the harbour, the moon was a brilliant silver beacon in the sky as it glowed down upon us. At any other time it would have been a beautiful night.

Raki turned to me, sitting on his horse with the raven on his shoulder, his wild white hair and beard illuminated by the great disk in the sky. He looked like a God, I thought!" Ari chuckled softly, scratching his whiskered chin, he shook his head. "Not a God though, just a man, a man with vengeance in his heart. He told me never to relent, that when all has been taken from you and your heart is as cold as stone there is naught else left but revenge for the one who caused your pain. He told me that though there would be many to try and dissuade you from your path you must stay true, for what vengeance could his wife and children take when they were dead and cold in the earth?

I understood a little of his pain, but not enough of it to tell him so. I would have dishonoured him if I had, I was a foolish boy with a broken heart not a warrior with blood on my hands… not yet."

"Im sorry…" Liv whispered but Ari did not hear her.

"We rode on for weeks. We practiced our sword play and I learned more about Raki. He told me of his past, a Viking raider and then a trader when he took his wife and she bore him sons, he told me of the Jomsvikings and urged me to take the path of a warrior than a family. I was swept up in the idea of blood fury and warring, of battling men, and releasing my rage, I had walked away from our home and left the boy Ari there. Now I was a man who had seen and done much, I was changed, it was easier to become like Raki.

My skills grew, he was pleased with me, and though he was a hard taskmaster, he knew too how to laugh and often goaded me with his humour. He was a friend and a father, but he needed no son only a man who could kill as well as he. It was as if the bird Muninn knew it, it was as if it reflected all the darkness in Raki's heart, always perched on his shoulder watching me and waiting. Raki could feed it and had trained it to hunt quarry when we needed meat, but for me it did nothing. Once I held it on my forearm, its claws digging into my flesh, Raki laughed at my discomfort and I wanted nothing but to shake it from gripping me.

It happened by chance that we were riding along a beach, at a slow pace for the morning was calm and we had lost the trail of the man. I learned his name was Ulfur. Suddenly Raki pulled his horse's reins and sat staring ahead, in the distance I saw men on horseback. One man was wearing a cloak concealing his features but Raki recognised him at once, it was Ulfur. Screaming a war cry from his throat Raki was seized by blood fury and sped his horse to the group. I chased after him readying my axe, I saw it happen too quickly. Raki sliced with his long sword through two of the men, their blood spraying onto the sands, they stumbled clutching the gaping wounds about their chest and neck. Lurching and screaming they fell into the seawater turning it red.

Ulfur jumped from his horse and readied himself for Raki's attack, but it was a trap, more men appeared from the dunes and surrounded Raki. I stopped and jumped down from my horse calling Raki, but he did not respond. He stood there poised to leap at Ulfur who had retreated beyond the circle of men. Raki swore and thundered foul curses at the men who were all heavily armoured, I ran and burst through the circle of men to join him. Muninn flew above our heads cawing and screeching when one of the men shot an arrow at him and he fell to the ground.

Raki seemed to snap from his ire and his face grew slack when he saw the bird land on the sand, it did not move. I shouted at Raki to move, to raise his sword arm, screamed and shouted for him to waken from his dream. Ulfur took his chance and swung a deathly blow with his axe from behind. Raki stumbled forward into my arms and dropped onto the sand, his blood flowed around my feet, he looked confused and shocked then understood he was dying. He pulled my ear to his mouth and whispered his final words. I understood.

Ulfur had begun to laugh, he grumbled with a dry crackled voice that he had ended the feud, the men around him stood sheathing their weaponry and sharing dark glances with one another. They were all dressed alike and wore hardened grim expressions. Ulfur sneered at Raki's dead body and from within his cloak retrieved a coin purse and threw it at one of the men. I realised then what they were, mercenaries, paid for to protect Ulfur and dispatch of Raki. Hired men.

I stood gripping my axe, I pointed it at Ulfur, I told the snake he was vile. I told him he had no honour, for what kind of man killed from behind? I challenged him to Holmgang there and then. Ulfur tried to back away but the men would not allow it. With no more than two blows from my axe I killed him, severed his head from his shoulders, watched him fall beside Raki's dead body. One of the men shouted 'Swift-Axe!' and thus I became Gorm Swift-Axe."

"Muninn…"

"Ja, Muninn. It appeared my slaying of his masters killer had not been enough. The men told me to join them and I did for what else was there for me to do? But first I buried poor Raki in the dunes. Then I went to Muninn's body, the arrow still sticking out of his breast. He did not flinch when I pulled the arrow from him but as I lifted his body he let out a final screech and clawed my jaw and neck, his fury at Raki's killing at last appeased. Then he was dead and I was bleeding. The raven had only ever been loyal to Raki. I buried Muninn beside Raki and cursed the feathered demon's name as I dug into the sand with my bare hands.

By this time the men had gathered their horses and grown impatient with my delaying them. I took my own horse and we left. One night before we reached their compound a man approached me, he had ointment to soothe and disinfect the wounds that should have been stitched but none were competent and I wouldn't allow them near my bare neck, the man told me of the nature of birds. He said 'they are unlike other animals, they have no loyalty to man, their spirits are free never to be tamed'. I told him that Muninn had been faithful enough to Raki, but the man shook his head and said 'it is not its nature it would have left him eventually'."

The small fire had all but nearly died out and though there was a coolness to the evening air Ari decided to let it dwindle to ash. Liv was covered in his sleeping fur and warm enough, he did not want to alert any that might be nearby they had arrived yet. Knowing he should rest before setting off at first light Ari lowered onto his back, closing his eyes for a moment.

"A good story, Ari… Raki will know peace with his wife and children… mayhap Muninn sits on his shoulder yet?"

"Hah!" Ari smiled wryly in the darkness of the hut. "Mayhap, when next I see that bird I will pluck every feather from his carcass!"

"Odin would be displeased…" Liv sighed.

Gradually her breathing became heavier realising she was sleeping Ari released a tight breath from his chest. He was glad she had come to for a time and spoken with him. Gytha had warned him to watch for signs that her mind was becoming muddled or if nonsense should fall from her lips that the elixir should be administered. She had also told him that the daudr sovn might prevent Liv from stirring at all and Ari wondered if he had dreamt it. Sleep eluded him for the rest of the night, fearing she might pass in her slumber, he listened to every wavering breath or labored sigh.

In the morning he was startled to find her skin had taken on a greyer hue and her lips were blue. As he lifted her onto Grani's back her body was limp and somehow weighed less than the previous day. A sweat glistened on her brow, but try as he might to moisten her lips with water, she would not drink from the skin. With his jaw firmly set Ari pulled Grani into a march towards the settlement. Leading the way to the forest, he picked his way along the woodland paths ever watchful and vigilantly aware of the danger of wolves.

Pushing the horse to his limits Ari reached the settlement before noon, hours before he had even hoped to, looking down onto the collection of longhouses cattle sheds and outhouses he saw the bodies of his people turn towards him. They were going about their duties preparing for the day when all at once the door of the hall flew open and the form of a man appeared. It was his uncle the Chieftain. Raising his sword arm, he shouted a welcome and beckoned Ari recognising at once the young man who had left six long years ago.

Ari felt a surging of hope well from within, he had returned and his family was still here. But as he walked down from the edge of the forest, to the clearing before the settlement nestled in a narrow valley, he saw another figure emerge from the hall and follow his Uncle to greet him. Ari swallowed the rage that threatened to erupt, he must remain calm, for it was the man he knew had betrayed Liv and who Ari now found himself delivering her to.

# 12.

Ove recognised his nephew at first sight, he had been aware that his arrival was coming, the old Seer had seen to that. He did not like the turn of events that had brought the man back into their midst, but was powerless to do anything about it. The sight of Ari quelled his thoughts for a moment until he saw the body of a woman across the back of the horse he led.

Waving to Ari he welcomed him into the settlement, but he could feel the Seer behind him, hovering like a gadfly around a cow in the summer sun. A chill crept across Ove's skin. Turning to the old man he glared at him furiously.

"So he has returned." Ove growled.

"Ja, as I told you he would, when I gave him the task I knew he would find her."

"And as I have told you should harm befall them or my people here it will be your head in the earth. We once welcomed you but those days are gone, your trickery and deceit saw to that."

The old man narrowed his dark steel blue eyes, his lips split in a snarl and he glared back with venom at the Chieftain. "For years you have prospered, I've done nothing to change that, don't be so foolish to think there isnt more in the world than your little island. Have I not been good to you? Healed your people, foreseen storms and disease, asked naught…"

"Tis true… you asked for naught but took anyway. Here comes my brother's son, mayhap we leave our discussion until you have spoken?" Ove shrugged off the man's cold look and strode towards Ari.

The old man turned on his heel and made for his chamber in the longhouse attached to the hall. He had seen the body across the back of the beast. His heart thudded at the thought she might be dead, but he had felt no such passing and could almost hear her breathing. Surmising she was injured, he swore under his breath, gathering his medicines and the scroll he had used once before, he took a breath. He knew this was going to be difficult. The bear Ove had proven himself to be no fool, his secrets were being exposed one by one and reuniting with Liv would cause further problems. He knew not what had happened to her in the last six years, more importantly; he had to know about the ring and the boy. He sat on his pallet for a moment, thinking dark thoughts.

Ove was a large strong man, he was the elder of three brothers, though only he and Ari's father still lived. His long hair was still as full and bright as a young mans but his face bore the brunt of wear and tear in the hot summers and long cold winters. His nose had been broken once too often and sat crookedly on his square face. Clean shaven, he smiled with a full set of teeth, his eyes clear and sharp, though oddly colored one being blue and the other brown. When he was a child his mother and father feared it was an omen their son was not meant for the world of Midgard, but Ove had shown them he was as strong and wise as any Chieftain's son should be.

The departure of Ari had been like a swift kick to the ribs from a mule, he had often thought his brother's son would take up the mantle of the settlement's leader one day. Ove had no sons of his own, though he loved his wife and their daughter dearly.

The flat worn earth of the yard crunched beneath his boots as he reached his nephew and wrapped his bear-like arms around him. He saw the changes in Ari, he saw the strain on his face and the scars on his neck. He felt the strength of a full grown man in his arms and not the sinewy limbs of the boy he had known. This man had fought and killed, his nature was changed but still it was his Ari.

"He is not trusted here but be wary of how you react." Ove whispered into Ari's ear. "Ho! Come and see, tis Ari returned to us! Fetch my brother, fetch his wife, we will feast tonight!" Ove then shouted to the gathering group of villagers.

The women clasped their hands in delight before running into the hall and setting to work in the kitchen. Children jumped and whooped at the display of their Chieftain chasing their dogs and running here and there in the yard. Men who had known Ari looked surprised and then shouted for joy before nodding respectfully and returning to their work. All had seen the body slung over the back of Grani, but none pursued an answer, assuming only Ari had brought a slave or prisoner with him.

"Ove tis Liv, I must see the Seer!" Ari jerked his head to the horse.

"Ja, ja, but Ari none must know she is here yet." Ove hushed Ari with a wave of a large hand. Taking Grani's reins, he led the horse to the barn near the great hall. "My boy, my boy!" Ove slapped Ari on the shoulder before turning to Liv and lifting her down.

Taking a breath Ove stared hard at the woman. "What sickness is this?"

"The daudr svon."

"What?! Nei it cannot be so!" Ove laid Liv on a loose mound of hay and stared up at his nephew. "You are well?"

"Ja, my parents?"

"Well… they will be here soon, they were at the farm and knowing your mother she will be flying down the hillside with your father on her heels." Ove stood folding his arms across his chest. "She is much changed, how came you by her?"

"I was sent by the Jarl, but before that word came to my Captain in the compound, I knew it was her. He warned me."

"He is a snake."

"Ja, but Liv knows naught… there was no time to tell her. How come you distrust the man now?"

"Six years is time enough to learn such things, think me a fool not to wonder about her going missing and he at the same time? I have heard stories about our Seer, I sent a man on their trail, this you would have known if you had stayed." Ove tried unsuccessfully to disguise the bitterness in his voice, seeing Ari wince at the remark he sighed. "I sent the same man to find you." He paused. "There is much we will speak of. But first we must take her to him, he will be in the longhouse, conceal her face when you carry her. I have no plans to explain this to anyone yet."

Just as Ari lifted Liv over his shoulder a man burst into the barn and stood in the doorway. He stood as tall as Ari and as broad and square faced as Ove. His tunic was rolled up at the sleeves and his hands muddied from working the earth that morning.

"Ari!"

Slowly a broad smile crept over Ari's face, his father stood before him. "Ja."

"My son!" Ari's father Ebbe stepped towards him joy threatening to explode from his chest, but halted, seeing the body slung over his son's shoulder. Nodding, he looked to Ove and glanced outside the barn door. Beckoning the men they left the shed and walked towards the longhouse. Ebbe would welcome his son home later.


The dream overtaking Liv caused her breathing to increase rapidly. She stood on the rainbow bridge, staring across the divide to Asgard. It was the most beautiful structure she had ever laid sight upon. Hewn from the wood of great oak trees the bridge was a myriad of carvings, great beasts wrestled with dragons, splinters of wooden fire erupting from their snouts. Intricate runes were carved over the boards of the walkway causing Liv to think of the markings on her skin. The bridge was covered in a layer of ice that gave it the appearance of glowing in the blackness surrounding her.

A man was standing next to her wearing a thick grey cloak made of wool and a mantle of grey wolf skin across his shoulders. He was pointing the way signalling her to take the long walk but she could not move. Her heart told her it was not yet time, she had to return for Ei and for Ari.

The man beside her took her forearm and brushed a hand across her forehead. He was tall and had the strangest eyes she had ever seen, they appeared to be made of molten lava, the irises a deep red swirling and moving as they bored into her opal gaze.

"You know me?"

"Ja, you are Heimdallr the watcher of Bifrost the rainbow bridge, you can see into the nine realms and hear all that is said and unsaid. You are a son of Odin the All-Father."

"You are the guardian of my father's line in Midgard, he awaits the day the boy will return. Why have you come alone?" His voice was low and hard.

"I became sick, I must return for Eileifr…"

"You have hidden the child, he is safe for now." The man looked away across the Bifrost as if listening to something in the distance. "Ja, there is naught to fear at present."

Taking a step away from the God with the frightening stare Liv drew a breath only to realise she no longer felt tired or ill. Heimdallr circled her staring all the while.

"Fear does not suit you, why are you afraid now?" He asked her whispering into her ear.

Shrinking away from the God Liv turned to face him taking another step to increase the space between them. "I have never met a God, have I angered you?"

"Are you so sure you have never met one?" Heimdallr frowned. "None are angry with you here."

For a moment Liv tried to understand what he meant but could not tear her gaze from his face, it was proud and stern. "Will you let me return?"

"Ja, you must for the boy." Suddenly the dark night sky that had surrounded them broke into millions of twinkling stars. Each one fell from the sky and landed at their feet, creating a blanket of tiny sparkling lights. "Gimli has awoken."

"The heaven's?"

"You will go there Liv, but not today, my father struck his staff into the ground to shake the stars from the sky, see he stands at the end of the bridge." Heimdallr continued to stare into her eyes, but pointed to a figure in the distance. "Tis time for you to go, but first…"

Taking Liv's hand Heimdallr took her to the edge of the rock they stood upon where Bifrost started, peering over the edge the God pointed down to a swirling mass of mist and water that stretched as far and as deep as Liv could fathom. Suddenly Heimdallr turned her wrist over tracing the line of runes circling her skin.

"You have been marked? These runes are spells, but this… what is this on your shoulder?" The God laid his palm flat on her shoulder blade before jerking his touch away as if his skin was burned. "That is a mark made by mortals who do not understand Yggdrasil, no God would allow the life giving tree to be burned upon the flesh."

"It was made by my guardian, but he is gone now, I will have no answers from him." Liv shrugged her shoulder away and followed the frowning gaze of the man before her.

"There." Said Heimdallr, looking intently at her once more and pointing to a formation in the mist. "There is Hornelen, and Smols, and there is the hall in which you lay barely alive. There is the one who will betray you at all costs, but for now he is saving you. He is the danger, he wishes not for the safety of the boy he wants only what he thinks he can gain from."

"The ring." Liv whispered. Her eyes strained as she looked down upon the rising images of the places and people she knew. Tears of rage burned her eyes and set her throat on fire. She saw what she could not believe and feared her mind was a broken as her body had become, she could not understand the images in the mist and turned away from the edge of the bridge.

"Ja the ring, you know it is cursed? Made from the ashes and tears of the Gods when one of their own was killed. The strong and good of heart can carry it, but it is worthless Liv."

"Nei…" She breathed in disbelief. "It cannot be…"

Heimdallr reached out and grasped her shoulder, Liv's head shot up and she straightened her back, her will was still strong she would not be afraid. Leaning to whisper in her ear, he spoke. "I have a secret for you…"

As Heimdallr spoke Liv felt every muscle in her body tense. Her hands felt as heavy and a lead weight but she clenched her fingers tightly digging her nails into the skin of her palms. Even here in the world of the Gods, she felt her blood surge and boil in her veins with fury. When at last Heimdallr finished, he turned her to face him.

"Ja, you are afraid no longer for it is not in your making Liv. You are a protector and fear will betray you. Know that I am always watching and listening, when it appears that all others have turned away or cannot come to you, I will. Now go and do what my father knows you must."

"My thanks." She nodded. "I have an ask of you."

"Then ask."

"Why did the All-Father ever need me? Surely he can save his child without me?"

Heimdallr closed his eyes and took a heavy breath. Looking back across the Bifrost he drew his heavy grey cloak about his shoulders. "There are nine realms, Midgard is the world of men and so you must be allowed to live as such, the Gods cannot upset the balance. Sometimes we walk among you as men and women, sometimes we take the form of birds or beasts. Mortals have a short life Liv, you must be allowed to live it, the fates work differently for us all. There is a purpose and a reason in all things."

"Is there peace at all in the future?"

"Nei Liv, not for Gods and not for men. But know that the life you live is precious and the one you protect more so. The boy is born from the love we lost when one of our own died, it was another son of Odin, who gave us hope again but this you already know. Call my name when you need me most and you will hear my horn thunder across the heavens. Go now, they are waiting for you." Heimdallr lifted the hood of his cloak over his head, concealing his deep garnet eyes and slowly made his way across the bridge, his arms folded across his chest, his feet leaving a trail through the fallen star dust.

A warmth spread over Liv's body, opening her eyes to the soft amber glow of the wooden panelled chamber she saw a figure leaning over her. Her eyes were weak and her vision blurred. A smell of burning incense filtered its way to her nose and then a sharper unpleasant smell replaced it. Sitting up suddenly she coughed and a hand that had been wavering a vial under her nostrils retreated swiftly. Her vision cleared and shock struck all noise from her throat.

It could not be, her mind raced, the dream had warned her but her mind was muddled. The face before her was grim and set, the figure's hair bound at his nape. His long beard trailing down his chest, his nimble fingers clenched in a fist before him. The surprise knocked her momentarily and her arms slipped back onto the furs. Slumping she raised her head once more to make certain of the man now coming closer leaning over her once more.

"My girl… my girl." He whispered.

"Don't get too close… step away." The voice of another man fell from the shadows across the room. Liv sensed the owner rise and stand behind the man, it was Ari who spoke she knew. "I'm warning you Seer." Ari growled at the man's back.

Liv massaged her temple and shook her head slightly. She was trying to make sense of what her eyes told her, but how it could be she did not know. But now the dream made sense, what Heimdallr had whispered in her ear, she remembered, and her deep anger replacing the fear that had threatened to creep in. She was strong, she must remember, she had survived and protected her charge even lying to Ari about Ei's death.

"How is it you stand before me after all this time?" Her voice rasped and then she spoke his name. "Harvardr?"

# 13.

The silence in the room was deafening. Ari looked upon Liv as she rose unsteadily from the pallet, her hair was loose and hanging over her shoulders, her grey dress was crumpled and the traditional brooches and apron missing. She looked bedraggled and almost like the thrall women of the village. Anger rose in Ari's throat, she was more than a slave and yet this man met her after all these years seeing her as not the survivor she was.

Liv squared her shoulders, taking a deep breath, she straightened her back and looked defiantly at Harvardr. At full height she was nose to nose with the old man. The bruising on her face had subsided to mere shadows, her skin had returned to a healthy glow and her eyes burned fiercely. Clenching her jaw Ari saw the muscles tick beneath the skin, she was enraged and trying hard to bury it he thought. 'Good!' Ari silently praised her, for she had to be strong, to show weakness in front of the man who had betrayed her would serve to hurt her further.

Harvardr looked at the woman and saw more than the girl he had trained, more than the being he had manipulated, he saw too she had gained wisdom. She was no longer the naive daughter of a slave who had believed his words so easily. 'Damn her!' his mind raged, for how was he to deal with her now, he had not been prepared for this. He had assumed that the world would have treated her harshly without the protection of a man for the last six years. He had reasoned a meeker woman to be standing before him, mayhap she would have hardened her emotions having to do what she must to survive but this woman had strength.

"Speak!" She directed her command to Harvardr through clenched teeth. She glared at the man, her hands trembling in balled fists at her sides. It was indeed her guardian, he was older and somewhat frailer looking but that was all on the surface. She now knew what lay beneath his leathery skin. He had the heart of a viper.

"Your anger is misdirected." Harvardr stepped away and placed his vial of rancid potion back within his pouch on the chest by the pallet. A small oil lamp burned on the chest top causing wisps of black smoke to filter up toward the thatched roof. "You are alive now because I healed you."

"How did you survive?"

"Survive? Ah, you mean the attack from the Jarls men?" Harvardr pulled a small wooden stool from a corner of the room and lowered stiffly onto it. His tunic was a dark brown dyed by the women in the settlement. Its rich wool was soft and felt good against his skin, but his feet ached in the rough boots he wore that were in need of repair and as the rains had not yet fallen he had neglected to do so. He had been so very busy with travelling to Smols and preparing for the return of Liv and Ari. Now his bones ached and his joints were swollen, the skin on his back felt soothed by the garment.

"Brodr died, he was a good man, he didn't have to die. Why didn't you?" Liv whispered the words watching the old man rub his aching fingers together. She saw the discomfort of age, but didn't care. She was standing a bedraggled mess before her enemy while he sat clothed well and his cheeks were not hollow with hunger. Turning to face him and draw his attention fully she leaned in slightly. "They slaughtered him, the Jarls men, but he didn't say a word. I hid with Ei, my hand over his mouth to stop him from screaming, and when at last they had hacked every limb from Brodr's body we ran. But where were you? There were bodies littered everywhere, women children, men but not yours. Do you know the guilt I carried thinking your corpse had been left to perish? Then after a time I feared the Jarl had you locked away in some pit, rotting with your heart still beating."

Harvardr tensed at the imagery Liv cast with her story. Of course he knew what had happened to Brodr, he had arranged it all. But he would not admit it to her, especially not with the looming presence of the Jomsviking in the room. "We were separated Liv, I searched for you but never found you. Then after many years there was thread, just a whisper at first, you had been seen… but you were alone. A trader on a ship talking of a woman who had hired him to sail for her, it was his son who had loose lips, he had seen strange markings on your skin and thought you a witch. I knew then you were alive, I knew then I was only weeks behind you." Harvardr stroked his long beard with his talon like fingers.

"There is some truth in that part." Ari growled. He was standing next to Liv, his hands tucked into his leather belt, across his back his heavy sword was still strung in its strap. Harvardr noticed the rich royal blue of his Jomsviking tunic and snorted in disgust. "It was then he sent a messenger to the compound for me telling of your sighting, he knew I would come. After speaking with my Captain I discovered that Jarl Brynjar had also been made aware." Ari directed a glance at Liv. "But for all your schemeing Harvardr you forgot to weigh the measure of a man, you did not think that there would be forgiveness rather than wrath. Had you imagined me delivering her to you bound with rope and shackled with chains?"

"You were not to reveal yourself!" Harvardr spat.

"Why? To deceive me further?" Liv shouted.

"To protect Ei! To hide the ring, these are your tasks Liv! What good would it have done to realise the man before you was Ari? Better it would have been that you discovered all here and felt warmth in your heart rather than then rage I see in you now! You accuse with your stares, believing I have lied, vent your fury towards me if you wish, but make sure it is justified!" Harvardr jabbed a pointed gnarled finger towards Liv and sneered. "You have come here without the boy, where is he? And the ring? I know you cannot have lost both for the God's would have smote you, by Odin I will do it myself! Nothing matters more than the child and the ring."

Slowly Liv lowered herself to her knees, staring directly at Harvardr eye to eye. "No more lies, I know full well the truth, you have nevered cared for Ei. All you ever wanted was the ring and you thought you had it did you not? The night of the attack Brodr presented me with two brooches. One concealing the ring and the other an empty copy. When the men attacked I was knocked out by a blow to the head, I thought it one of his men mistaken in my identity... nei, it was you. I came too and found Ei crying in the corner of the blacksmiths forge. We hid as I said until it was safe. When next I had my wits and we had run far enough, I discovered one brooch was missing. Tell me Harvardr how enraged were you and Brynjar to discover you had the wrong one? No ring, no child, no trail for you to follow."

Ari felt as if his mind were about to explode, what kind of treachery was this? The old Seer had been at work for some time, but his deeds were of the worst kind, a terrible violation of trust and honour.

"Why would I have done such things Liv?" The Seer asked, cocking his head and a vacant expression in his eyes.

"Because you grew to hate what you had been tasked with. You were severed from your own kind, lumbered with a legend and a child, you had tried to barter your way out of the task before I realise that now. With Brodr and his Chieftain father, you wanted rid of us but craved the wealth of the ring. You betrayed us to Brynjar to gain  wealth and that man who has chased me relentlessly for the last six years was mad and insane enough to be swept away by your words. Did he torture you when you failed? Or is this your chance at retribution? Or did you run and hide from him waiting and listening for my whereabouts to try and strike again?"

"You have become a vile woman." He snapped.

"If I have then it is praise to you!" Liv stood breathing evenly and calmly.

"Tell me of the ring, tell me of the boy!" Harvardr's voice crackled under the torment of frustration caused by the woman. He felt defeated and it did not suit him to feel much of anything he did not like.

"At last, you ask for the one thing you wanted more than anything firstly... the ring? Thrown into the ocean before I was captured. And Ei? For that is his name... not boy. Never... never will I tell you." With her final words Liv walked to the small chamber door, sliding the wooden latch, she left the room and paused in the hall. She saw two men standing opposite the doorway, their arms folded and grim expressions on their faces. Moving past them she paused a little farther along the passageway. Moments later, Ari joined her.

"He will be set under guard in a room out of sight. You did well."

"I need air. We are in Ove's longhouse?" Resting her head against the rough wooden panels of the wall, she wondered if it would be best to hide herself away from the sight of the villagers. Her energy had been expended and she felt weak once more.

"Would be best you get rest but come with me, I have little time before I must fetch the others from the lake. They left behind us… you know you were close to death?"

"Ja I dreamt as much." Liv nodded and turned to face him. "Ari you must go I will rest in another room, mayhap speak with Ove? Your parents are well?"

"Ja. Come you must see something new and it is safe." Taking her elbow Ari led her out of the hallway running between the longhouse and the great hall of Chieftain Ove. Taking a side step they passed through the back of the hall and out into a small grassy yard. A small bench was secluded in a corner with a low overhanging roof to provide shelter. The yard was enclosed by wattle and daub fencing. Seeing Liv's confusion Ari gestured to the bench and sat beside her.

"Three years or so ago Ove's daughter gave birth to twins, she was much sickened afterwards and had little strength to walk, Ove had this small yard made so that she might play with the boys as they grew. She is well now, but for a time not even the other women could approach her without her contracting some illness. Ove says she is now so strong she takes the boys with her and her husband everywhere, sailing, climbing, she will not be confined again." Ari chuckled. "But mayhap that is just a tale for I see a drinking horn resting near your foot, mayhap my uncle hides here to drown his thoughts when has angered my Aunt!"

"Hah, so there is!" Liv nudged the horn with the soft leather of her boot.

"The child is alive then?" Ari asked.

"Ja, he is." Liv closed her eyes, letting Ei's small laughing face fill her mind.

"We must talk of it."

"Ja." She sighed.

The sun began to set on the last of the warm summer days, gnats darted here and there in the long grass and birds flew overhead, Liv felt a sense of return to her old home. Relaxing she let her back lean against the wall of the house and breathed in the sweet air. Her skin began to cool and the aching that had been so present in head was almost gone completely.

"He read from a scroll, runic inscriptions, in our old tongue. The tongue of the God's. But you did not make it easy for him, what did you dream of?" Ari asked.

"Damn him and his magic! I dreamt I was talking with…" Just at that moment the sound of a horn in the distance reverberated through the trees and across the fields.

Jumping to his feet Ari cursed. "Dag!" Turning quickly to Liv he motioned for her to stay put. "I must go, he would only blow the horn if need be, stay I will send Ove for you."

Nodding in agreement Liv watched Ari disappear with haste into the longhouse. She wanted to tell him to ride safely, that she hoped the others had not come to harm, she had wanted to thank him. Feeling weak once more she gripped her hands together, a memory from her dream broke her thoughts and the sound of the horn rang in her ears.

"I remember Heimdallr." She whispered. For the moment she was safe, she had no need to call his name and it was not his horn that had rung from the skies.

Thorik at once realised his mistake, dropping Dag's horn he backed away from the Jomsviking's pack. The men had separated and headed in opposite directions, securing their position. They had arrived at the lake of Smols and found the beaten and ramshackle goat herder's hut. Dag found little evidence that anyone had occupied the hut recently save for the hoof prints left in the soft earth by Grani.

On hearing the horn sound his head shot up from his crouched position, he had been sweeping a gaze back and forth along the line of the trees. Now and then he glanced to Holger who was doing the same on the other side of the body of water. Then he saw the Jarls man stand and run in the direction of Gytha and the boy. Dag sprang onto his feet and broke into a sprint reaching them moments before Holger.

Gytha was waving her hands at the men calming them before they approached but it did little to soothe Dag's temper.

"By the God's!" Dag glared at Thorik who stood behind Gytha.

"There is no harm Dag, please he was curious, I should have kept an eye on him better!" Gytha spoke quickly.

"Get from behind her skirts boy!" Holger shouted.

Feeling ashamed and embarrassed Thorkil stepped forward puffing out his chest. All at once his bravado expired and he resorted to pulling at his tufted hair. "I just wanted to see if I could." He lamely explained.

"You blew the Jomsvikings horn? Madness!" Holger was exasperated, throwing his hands up into the air he let them fall and slap his sides. "You have alerted all to our location, why even the goats at the top of the mountain will know where we are!"

"Nei! It wasn't that loud!" Thorik took a breath, feeling hurt by Holger's anger. 'Why is he not proud I have shown I could make it sing?' he wondered 'Tis not an easy task!'

Reading Thorik's thoughts Dag rolled his eyes and strode over to the boy. Grabbing his arm, he shook him roughly. "You have shown your lungs are strong, but your curiosity has endangered us all. Who is to say who or what is lurking on our trail? If we are attacked am I to protect you or let you fight?"

"Fight!" Thorik whispered.

"Nei, Gytha here would have to take you and hide. You are foolish Thorik, you were when first we met and you have continued to be so!"

"But… Holger I brought him to you he is here to help, and Grani I brought him to you also! I'm not foolish Dag I want to fight to be a man to…"

"Blow a Jomsvikings horn?" Gytha smiled at the boy feeling

sorry for him. Since he was only a boy, albeit one that had led a sheltered existence. He was not at all what she imagined Dag, Ari and Holger had been like as children. But the men were right, they might be watched at this moment and she feared the danger of the possibility. However, something told her with Ari's settlement close by there was really only the smallest chance that some of the Jarl's men had been able to follow their trail. Even if they had, they were a few days behind them.

Holger stepped forward crouching before the waif-like child. "You were lucky I saw sense and accompanied you here, but just as easily I could have been a threat Thorik. Remember when we spoke by the fire? I saw something in you that made me take a chance, please think with your head and make me not regret what I have done." He spoke softly as if any further anger would wound the boy terribly.

Releasing Thorik's arm Dag nodded at Holger, walking over to his pack he lifted the horn and attached a long thin strip of leather around the mouthpiece. Satisfied the loop was fastened he glanced at Thorik and beckoned him over. "Here, I give you the horn, but do not feel tempted to blow it again… unless by my command, understand?"

Enthusiastically Thorik nodded, but waited until Dag presented the horn to him before grabbing it with both hands marvelling at the prize.

"Besides, you make is sing better than I can!" Dag shrugged. He watched as the boy traced his small thin fingers over the wavering lines and circles of the bone. It wasn't a large horn, especially precious to him or as intricately decorated as some he had seen, but the boy had been drawn to it and he was happy it had been that rather than his axe sword or Daggers.

Standing Holger walked over to Thorik and pulled him away, telling him to gather moss, leaves and kindling to start a small fire. He caught Dag's eye and squinted in appreciation of the gesture. Satisfied that the boy was busying himself Holger joined Dag and Gytha by the water's edge.

"Think we are watched?"

"Nei, not by men, just the woods." Dag grunted kicking small pebbles into the lake.

"The woods?" Gytha shivered at the thought.

"Creatures Gytha, naught more than that, a fire will keep them at bay." Dag reassured her and watched as she walked over to Thorik. The boy had managed to light a small fire and was feeding it twigs while crouching on his haunches. The horn still strapped around his back.

"He dreams of becoming a Jomsviking." Holger said.

"He would not if he knew what that meant." Dag replied dryly.

"Thank you for giving him the horn. It will make him feel brave, worthy."

Dag stared at the man. He was very tall and strong, a good ten years older than himself perhaps more he thought. He had a crooked smile that revealed teeth still strong and had not blackened with age. His hair was thick, straight and the color of a setting sun, the redness streaked with lines of white. The hair on his head seemed older than the face it crowned. Heavy deep lines ran along the man's forehead and around the creases of his eyes.

"He is stronger than he looks." Dag said, shrugging looking across the lake once more to the treeline.

"Please do not encourage him to join your kind. Once I knew a man who became a mercenary, he had a sad life and did not live long.

"My joining was necessity... the boy has choices, mayhap I encourage you to tell him it unwise to serve under the rule of vengeful Jarl?" Smirking, he saw the anger and then softening of Holger's features as he realised Dag was jesting with him.

Raising his thick eyebrows Holger turned and spat on the soft dark earth. "Hah! Done Dag, done!"

"You have left your family in Srovberget, did you not want to return to them first and take them to safety?"

"Nei it could not be done that way. I was days from them already and the moment I set foot in Srovberget the damned bastard Brynjar would know and send for me. His wrath at my failure would have been great, but I doubt he would have killed me. Mayhap he would have punished me in other ways involving my family. I do not want them to suffer."

Dag nodded at the explanation and believed what the man had told him. "Ja, this Brynjar has a reputation. Think he will follow us here, to this island? It is small and far enough away from his lands, he would need a ship for I believe the causeway is not known to all."

"He is well informed, there is a man he knows that has aided him in the past. Some kind of Seer I think. But they are not friends and I cannot be sure what the Jarl knows."

"Does Ari know of this?"

"I know not, there was not time to say much more other than warn you that Brynjar will find a way to locate you."

Wearily Dag rubbed his forehead roughly. "Then we must let fate decide what will happen."

Holger looked blankly at the man before him. "I will help you where I can and then ask you once more to help me, I will pay the coin I have enough."

Dag slapped Holger on the shoulder and directed him to walk towards Thorik Gytha and the fire. "What say we talk of your family when the worst of this is over. I do not relish the idea of the Jarl and his men on this island, truth be told I do not know what will become of you when he realises your severing of ties with him. Make it through that and we will talk more then."

Nodding Holger let the matter drop like a pebble thrown into a calm body of water. His hopes were not dashed completely, but now he feared the coiling of dread within his stomach. He was not sure whether to wish for the approach of the Jarl, he felt so inevitable or pray for them to rest.

# 14.

It had been early in the day when King Harald Greycloak's man had arrived in the hall of Jarl Brynjar. There had been no warning that the man would come and so his arrival had taken Brynjar by surprise which Solvieg instantly realised was the plan all along. It had only been a matter of time before Brynjar's negligence of his duties in attending the Thing at Gulafjord was noticed. Srovberget was tightly controlled and earned the King much coin, it was foolish of Brynjar to have behaved in such a fashion.

Solvieg stood beside her husband listening to the obligatory courtesies spoken among the men. She felt wary and afraid of the man's intentions, he was of breeding she suspected, tall, powerful and strong he stood taller than her husband and his presence more dominating. His eyes were sharp and bright, his face equally so, his clothing expensive and adorned with a mantle of rich animal fur over his shoulders. Only his boots betrayed the evidence of a journey made swiftly. The first of the rains had arrived turning the dry earth into a sodden myre of mud, the man had tracked it into her husbands hall. She eyed the trail of muck from the heavy wooden doors across the rush strewn flood to her husband's chair. Solvieg sighed at the thought of her servant women having to sweep the floors and start over again, she was fastidious in the hall's appearance whether Brynjar noticed it or not.

"Jarl Brynjar, my arrival seems to have unsteadied you, are you ill?" The man spoke without concern in a cool calm manner. A chill crept over Solvieg's skin.

"Nei I am well." Brynjar grunted. He sat with his thick, heavy hands placed upon his knees, leaning slightly forward in the great chair. Indeed, he appeared unwell, his skin was pale and his hair damp with sweat.

"Then you have another reason for not attending in Gulafjord?" The man queried before turning to his own men gesturing for them to take a seat on the benches around the long rectangular tables. Two men stayed at the King's man's side while the others all sat facing and staring at Brynjar. None had removed their weapons and none had taken up on the offer of ale and porridge served by the hall servants.

"My remaining in Srovberget is not intended as a slight to Greycloak…"

"Then what?"

"What?" Brynjar snapped his head up looking the man full in the face. He took a breath realising this was no mere guard, it was the son of Greycloak's oathbrother.

"You are not ill, you say no offence is intended, so I ask you why you are here?" The man furrowed his brow. Slowly he unfastened a heavily decorated brooch from his mantle and swung the heavy fur onto the table behind him. He quickly glanced at Solvieg as he did so. Although the summer was waning and the mornings noticeably cooler the fur was a statement more than a necessity. "Does it offend my lady that my men have trampled into her hall?"

"Tis my husbands hall, and no it does not offend me. My women will aide me in its repair later in the day." Solvieg tried her best to sound winsome and flighty but her voice trembled. She wished to appear as no more than a vain woman of Brynjar's, she wanted no attention brought to herself for her husbands nature could be cruel.

"Ja they will. Tell me… Solvieg how long have you been the wife of the Jarl?"

"Damn you! Address me and not my wife!" Brynjar roared, spittle flew from his mouth, standing suddenly he clenched a fist in the man's face. "She's a mere woman, naught more, you seek to embarrass me in my own hall?!"

"Ja!" The man roared back. Then stepping forward, he prodded a finger in Brynjar's chest. "I address the woman when I get no sense from her man! Answer me before I split you in two, why are not at the Thing? Why is it I arrive in Srovberget when I should be with my men in Gulafjord?!"

Brynjar staggered back a step, the backs of his legs touching the wooden frame of the great chair. Before he could answer the door of the hall opened and a man with a staff made his way to the men.

Solvieg gasped catching sight of her husbands glaring look he fired at her as she did so. The man with the staff walked awkwardly towards them, but his back was straight and his chin held high. It was Inge.

"Ah, finally we have one who might give me answers!" The King's man grunted. "Inge Agarsson! So this is your brother, only once I have met him before now, he made no impression on me and continues to do so."

The insult made Brynjar grind his teeth. It had been over a week since Inge had learned of his wife's and child's death, he had remained absent from the evening meals even at his brother's request he join. Inge knew it was only so Brynjar could rub salt in his fresh wounds. Solvieg had managed to get word to Inge about his family's deaths before the Jarl had had the full opportunity to twist the knife into his heart.

"Why are you here Inge?" Brynjar growled.

"I was sent for." Inge spoke but looked only toward Solvieg. The fact was not missed.

"My name since you did not ask is Rorik." The King's man interrupted. "Give me a reason before I continue Brynjar. Make it good."

"Continue with what?" Brynjar spat, his dark glare darting between his brother and his wife. His brow was beaded with perspiration caused by rage and his strange sickness that had grown. The tingling in his arm and fingers had turned to sharp spiking throbs of pain and his leg continuously ached. At night he could not sleep for the blinding headaches, no potions the healer woman could offer seemed to work.

Rorik turned to Inge and looked the man up and down. Inge was indeed crippled, but Rorik could see it had not affected the man's mind, his eyes were keen, bright and sharp like his brothers, but his face bore more honesty that Brynjar's had never had. Glancing at the woman Solvieg, he saw her worried eyes moving over the earthen floor, her lips were in a tight thin line on her oval face, her hair tightly braided. She looked like a woman who had heard the harsh edge of her husbands tongue once too often and perhaps more thought Rorik.

He felt some amusement in the torture he was bestowing on the Jarl, it pleased him this odious man was twisting and churning in his guts. He had met Brynjar before and like his father who was an oathbrother to King Harald Greyclock he had no love for him. It had been said that Brynjar would break his word, had intolerable greed and lately had shown signs of madness. Nothing Rorik had seen proved otherwise, the man was clearly not of his own mind, it was in the Jarl's eyes.

"Inge, how come you to be lame of leg?" Rorik queried solemnly.

"My horse was struck in battle, it fell and broke the bones in many places, it was not set properly and never returned to full strength." Inge narrowed his stare, holding his proud chin high, he hated his leg and the damned staff he was forced to use to right his body.

"Ah, then it is no malady from birth? Many a child is cast out for being a weakling, I myself gave my father cause for concern, but I grew strong and proved him wrong."

"I did not know that Rorik."

"Nei, can you walk unaided?" Rorik nodded at the staff, his arms now folded across his chest. The men behind him watching silently as Inge considered his answer, they knew it would be key as to what happened next.

"I can swing a sword, an axe, grapple with a man, but I will never run again and in the winter walking pains me. I have the leg it would have been worse if I had lost it." Inge replied shortly. Solvieg took a deep breath and glanced furtively toward her husband's brother.

"He is a cripple!" Brynjar stood angrily slamming his fist on the engraved armrest of the chair. "He could never hope to be a whole man again, tis by my good nature that he graces my hall to feast when he does naught to aide his Jarl. Nei, even his wife and child are dead such was his inability to care for them!" The hatred in Brynjar's voice was hot with rage.

But as Brynjar shouted his venom Rorik stood fast looking only at Inge. He saw the man listen to the vile words without flinching taking only a moment to let a wry smile form on his mouth before it was gone. Rorik licked his lips, preparing to speak, but it was Solvieg who spoke up.

"Husband, know this, Inge is no more responsible for the deaths of his wife and child than you are for the rising and setting of the sun and the moon. He is an honourable man, and this you cannot understand for honour has abandoned you completely. Be Inge a cripple or not he is still more a man worthy of a seat in Valhalla amongst his Gods and fellow warriors than you could ever be. He is your brother, your words should never have been said even if you think them to be true." Her eyes were brimming with tears.

Before any of the men in the room could react to Solvieg's words a loud crack broke the silence as Jarl Brynjar's palm whacked against his wife's face. Like a woman who had felt the sting of such a slap before she merely tilted her head away from her husband. Gently her fingertips touched the sight of the blow and against the pain she smiled.

"Every word she said was true, you have dishonoured yourself." With care Inge laid a hand on Solvieg's shoulder, his eyes searching her face. He saw a lone tear trail down her cheek over the red welt forming on her skin.

"If she had been lying, she might have deserved the humiliation Brynjar, but she was not." Said Rorik, his arms now unfolded and one hand resting on the sword strapped to his thick leather belt.

"You... you will call me Jarl in my hall!" Brynjar jabbed a thick finger toward Rorik. "Your playfulness of tongue has come to an end, speak your mind like a man and not a woman hell bent on trickery and slyness of words... I am Jarl here!"

"Ah... but you see Brynjar..." Rorik paused stoney faced. "You are not."

The King's men behind Rorik now stood forming a semi-circle behind their leader. Each was well armed though all of Brynjar's own men in the room sat stunned and immobile. They neither reached for their weapons nor stood to defend their Jarl. Brynjar took in the betrayal and it stuck in his throat like a fish bone.

"You have come here to displace me?!"

"Nei, you are stripped of your title, your lands and your wealth. You are banished from Srovberget, do not think to return, had the decision been mine or my fathers you would be dead. Did you think you could conceal the truth from Greycloak forever? You suffer from a weak mind and ill judgement on the company you keep. A messenger arrived confirming what we had long been suspected, your deception was revealed. King Harald Greycloak is your King, your word is bound to him only, and no other man not even his Uncle." Rorik glared at Brynjar watching as defeat and then fury distorted the man's features.

"So you cast me out over some rumour? Your suspicions? I have had some spy in my midst that has fed you falsehoods…"

"You mean to say you have not sworn allegiance to Bluetooth should he replace our King of Norway?"

"Wherein lies the treachery in that? Would not Greycloak himself swear fealty to his Uncle should this happen? Greycloak is his vassal!" Brynjar was grasping at straws.

"You plead ignorance at what I have said? You show stupidity by not hearing my words?" Rorik thundered. "We know that you have spoken of Greycloak's death… to make it clear to you Brynjar that is treason."

"Nei… this spy cannot be trusted!"

"It is you that cannot be trusted. We have a King of our lands! Harald Greycloak has fought many battles, he is the son of Eric Bloodaxe and the grandson of Harald Fairhair! Greycloak's Uncle would desire wealthy provinces such as Srovberget, you are telling me here in your hall that you have not given away your word in promise of wealth and power?"

"What?!" Brynjar snapped viciously. Could it be he had been betrayed? It could not be, his mind furiously raced at the idea, but it sounded as clear as the light of a summers day that this man Rorik knew something of the secret quest he was on. But perhaps it was not so secret after all, had he been foolish and absent in his handling of the situation he wondered. "This King Greycloak that the people seem too eager to call him with pride, is a man lustful for battle and extending his territories, he is watched carefully by Bluetooth for such a man might start a conflict not even he could survive!"

"You have lost your mind!" Rorik's demeanor slipped and he spoke the words viciously.

"Such blind loyalty! I watch my back as well your Greycloak should watch his! You speak of his battles, what of King Haakon's death at Fitjar? Is Greycloak so arrogant he thinks Haakon's son will not avenge him?" Brynjar slammed his mouth shut suddenly, he was on the verge of saying too much and knew it, he had already said enough to warrant death rather than banishment. It was not over for him yet, he had spilled his ire and now he would reign in his fury for he was perilously close to confirming Rorik's thought that he was mad.

"Your two brothers have turned down the right to your chair, no doubt they fear your retribution and but more likely they are aware of your dealings and those you are linked to." Rorik controlled his anger speaking as though he were talking to a simpleton rather than the conniving snake that stood before him. "But Inge here has proven to be an intelligent man, brave even considering what he takes on in your place. It is Inge who will now be Jarl and Solvieg's hand is also his. You will be escorted from the hall, take a pack and a horse, the blacksmith will provide you with a sword unlike one you have ever handled I suspect. No man will follow you, none would dare." Rorik flung a filthy glance to the still seated men of the former Jarl. None nodded in agreement but neither did they protest. Rorik knew a few would follow Brynjar but he cared not, they would never attempt a return if they did so. The rats nest must be cleared.

To Inge he spoke quietly as he took a few steps toward him. "This is your hall now, I hope Solvieg can heal what has been wounded, she is a brave woman to have spoken as she did. She could not have known what was to happen here and still she spoke for you. Treat her better than her former husband, I suspect you will."

Silently Inge nodded once, taking the offered forearm of Rorik he grasped it and shook it. He did not smile or show any signs that he felt anything at this moment when other men might have.

Solvieg stood staring at the two men, slowly, her gaze willed Inge's to meet her own. Inge said nothing, but took her elbow leading her away from Brynjar and out of the hall into the passageway of the longhouse.

The King's men relaxed sheathing their swords once again taking a seated position but still on guard. Rorik jerked his head at two of them who at once stood. "See to it he is given rough clothing to wear and have him watched in the stable, he will have an able horse but not one of his own fine stock. I will be with you to escort him from the gates. Allow no-one to speak with him."

The men approached Brynjar and roughly took him by each arm. At first he resisted digging his heels into the floor and swearing under his breath. Then all at once he stopped jerking and twisting his shoulders, taking a breath Brynjar leaned towards Rorik with a mean snarl on his lips.

"If I so offended the King why did he send such a thick headed bastard to tell me? Is he afraid? Ja that is it, he hides behind the men willing to do his bidding. Let him have this day for I will have many, many others, think you taking my title and my wealth is enough to stop me? Nei, I am a strong man and this is but a day I must end."

"It will end Brynar and tomorrow when another begins, I think even the God's will hear your cries of anguish. Now get you from my sight before I defy my father and Greycloak and split you in half where you stand!" Rorik spat on the man's face watching the spittle trail over his nose and chin. He would very much liked to have killed him, for though his father and Greycloak were hard taskmasters he was loyal to them and would have no man speak ill of them.

The guards took Brynjar from the hall without resistance, Brynjar's men sat looking at one another unsure of whom they were duty bound to serve. Rorik saw the hesitance in them and swore under his breath. Walking towards them, he again placed his hand on the hilt of his sword.

"You will swear fealty to Jarl Inge, failure to do so will not be well received. Should any of you decide to follow the traitor expect no better treatment than he has seen. Your lack of voice when the punishment was being read out tells me there is no strong love for your former leader. But know this, fail Inge in any way and I will return and set all your hides upon a pyre." With that, he turned and made his way to the passageway Inge and Solvieg had taken.

He knew they would be in the rear chamber that had belonged to Brynjar for he had told Inge to go there after the punishment had been dealt. Upon entering the room he saw Solvieg's distressed face and Inge sitting on a heavily decorated chair carved with dragons and all manner of beasts sent from Hel.

"You planned this?! Before Inge came you spoke? Why did no-one tell me?"

"I had to be sure you were trustworthy." Rorik spoke flatly at the woman. "When you said what you did about Inge I was satisfied, worry not Solvieg. Inge vouched for you, but it was I who had to know, I am sorry Brynjar struck you."

"You let him live after all he said? He is a traitor and you let him go? I do not understand." Solvieg sat on the edge of the fur lined bed, her head in her hands.

"Brynjar hides much Solvieg, we both know he would never give up names of those he has conspired with even under torture, he must think he has gotten away with his plans. He will be watched and we will learn more." Rising to his feet Inge stared at his new wife feeling grief for those he had lost and the new turmoil entering their lives.

"Inge is right Solvieg, now you must support your new husband and lead your people well. There is much strife in the land yet, Greycloak will push father to secure his lands and it is true that Bluetooth the Dane will come. Why would he not when Greycloak has been so successful, we know it, but it will do naught to hamper the future of Norway. Haakon's son will present himself at some point on that there is little doubt."

"Nei, nei… you do not see it all." Solvieg wept wiping the tears from her face, she drew a breath. "He is mad, all you have said is true and Inge I thought you would see it more, but all Brynjar has in his heart is the damnable legend. What you men strive for he will turn from, for it is not his true course. He will lead you not to spies and conspirators, he will leave this place and chase down the one thing he desires. The ring and the child, he will take the jewel and expect immortality, endless glory and wealth, and he will kill the child he believes to be the mortal line of Odin on earth! Your King, your politics, this land, it is nothing to him… in his lunacy he is focused on one thing only."

Both the men looked stunned, gripping his staff tightly Inge lowered his head and considered Solvieg's words. He had not believed in the legend thinking it a peculiarity of his brothers, dismissing that it was not in fact something all together much different and stronger for Brynjar.

"Every man believes in the God's. You cannot believe that Brynjar…" But Rorik was unsure what he really thought, could Brynjar be so twisted of mind he wondered.

"What we believe makes no difference." Said Inge slowly, sweeping his gaze around the room.

"No matter, he will be watched, there is nowhere for him to go, but to those he conspires with. Eventually he will reveal what we need to know even if he realises his actions or not." Rorik made for the chamber door but as he turned the wooden latch he heard Solvieg whisper under her breath.

"He will damn us all. He will lead you to nothing but the misery he wishes to inflict on those he seeks." She said.

"Solvieg he cannot harm us further. His quest will take him far from Srovberget, what is it you fear so much?" Inge's tone was firm but pained at the woman's distress.

"He will lead you all to Hel! Death must be the only punishment he see's. There will be no peace, where you think he cannot reach he will and his wrath will be most terrible. Ja he is a traitor and now his men see, but there are those who will follow him and kill for him and there are those who believe as strongly as he. Rorik please spill his blood, for if you do not this hall will burn and all who reside in it, Brynjar will see to that." Her throat constricted and Solvieg crumpled onto the floor. For one moment in the hall she had felt freedom from Brynjar, almost a sense of joy that now she was bound to Inge there may be some purpose to her life other than misery, but the realisation of her own words stung like nettles on her skin. She felt desolate and certain that Brynjar would yet have his day.

End of Part One

# Characters Places and Terms

Liv – Ei's protector, name has means protection and life
Gorm/Ari – Jomsviking, name means eagle
Dag – Gorm/Ari friend
Gytha – Tavern maid/healer
Harvardr – Seer, name means guardian
Eileifr – The child Liv protects, means heir, nicknamed Ei
Thorik – Fishermans son
Holger – Jarls captain
Jarl Brynjar – Jarl of Srovberget
Solvieg – Jarls wife
Inge – Jarls crippled brother
Ove – Chieftain of Smols
Ebbe – Ari's father
Lena – Ari's mother
Harald Greycloak – King of Norway
Rorik – Greycloaks messenger
Harlad Bluetooth – King of Denmark ad Greycloaks Uncle
Odin – The All-Father, leader of the Norse Gods
Heimdallr – The Watcher, Odin's son, surveys the nine realms
from the rainbow bridge Bifrost
Gulafjord – Township where the Thing is held
Srovberget – Jarls land
Giffni – Hot spring caves on the coast near Smols
Smols – Island of Bremenger (modern name) homeland of Ari and
Liv
Smalsarhorn – Hornelen seacliff
Hudfat – Hide and fur sleeping bag
Skald – Poet and storyteller
Seer – a practicer of magical arts
Seidr – magic used by the Gods and those who practice the art
Volur – female seers
Yggdrasil Kynslod – Group sworn to oversee the line of Odin and

protection to the line

Raindow Bridge - Bridge that reaches between Midgard (the world) and Asgard, the realm of the Gods

Midgard – The world of mortal men

Asgard – The home of the Gods